ATTRACTION OF OPPOSITES

"You wouldn't fit in here," Leitrim told her. "You'd be a fish out of water. Why don't you just enjoy the sojourn for what it is—a brief Arabian adventure."

"Perhaps you're right," she said consideringly. "But what's an adventure without some romance, Leitrim? You have your company business to employ your mind. My major business in life is to find the right man, and inveigle the poor unfortunate into marrying me. I am just going about my business."

"One could wish you had a wiser mentor than Miss Trimmer."

"She suits me very well. I can always wind her round my finger."

"Just as I feared," he said wearily. "It will be for me to play the role of tyrant."

"You play it exceedingly well, sir!"

Other Leisure books by Joan Smith:

DESTINY'S DREAM
EMERALD HAZARD

SILVER WATER, GOLDEN SAND

Joan Smith

LEISURE BOOKS   NEW YORK CITY

A LEISURE BOOK

April 1989

Published by

Dorchester Publishing Co., Inc.
276 Fifth Avenue
New York, NY 10001

Printed in the United States of America.

Chapter One

Lady Melora Worth looked around the ship's cabin, lifted her tea cup and sighed. "We might as well be having tea in any polite drawing room for all the excitement of this trip," she said.

Her chaperone lifted her eyes from a marble-covered gothic novel and smiled vaguely. Miss Trimmer's gray hair was covered by a wisp of lace, and a paisley shawl hung over her bony sloping shoulders. "Captain Redding has given us a very comfortable cabin," she agreed, smiling contentedly at the elegance of a striped sofa, mahogany sofa table and the silver tea set that adorned it. Miss Trimmer's main concerns in life were her comfort and her tea. Throw in a trashy, sentimental novel and she asked little more of fate. She had some rudimentary conscience, however, and tried to inculcate the maidenly virtues of deportment and *ton* into her charge.

1

Lady Melora's blue kid slipper bobbed up and down in impatience. Miss Trimmer spotted the motion and said firmly, "You're skittish as a cat on coals, Melora. A lady holds her posture steady. Furthermore, you display your ankle at every bob."

"There is nothing amiss with my ankle," the young lady replied pertly, and inclined her head to admire it. Indeed there was nothing amiss with Lady Melora's entire appearance. From the tip of her blonde curls to the toe of her dainty slipper, she was quite obviously an Incomparable. Long, sooty lashes enhanced her deep blue eyes. The dignity of a straight nose was diminished by her pouting lips and short chin. Her rose lute-string gown was in the latest Empire mode, cut rather low at the bodice, nipping in above the waist to fall free below.

"If only your manners matched your appearance," Miss Trimmer said, and shook her gray head ruefully. "In England, a lady needs more than a hefty dowry to nab herself a good *parti*, my dear."

"I don't see why we had to leave Bombay, just when I had attached a very eligible gentleman."

"Pshaw! A quill-driving clerk from the East India Company is no fit match for an earl's daughter. Your Uncle Gerard will expect you to look a deal higher than that, milady! First we go home to London, *then* you find a *parti*. You are always putting the cart before the wheel."

"Horse," Melora said.

"Precisely! The horse before the wheel."

Melora rolled up her eyes and said, "Charles was very handsome."

"Handsome is as handsome does. If you don't recognize a gazetted fortune-hunter when you meet one, it is my job to keep you away from disaster. Never mind tossing your shoulders in that underbred fashion, Melora. I swear you have picked up Indian manners."

Lady Melora set down her tea cup. "Is that not a contradiction in terms, Miss Trimmer? You have been telling me the past two years the Indians *have* no manners."

Miss Trimmer's eyes returned to her book as she arranged herself more comfortably. The jiggle of her shoulders called to mind a hen settling her feathers for the night. Lady Melora rose impatiently and began to pace the cabin. She went to the porthole and gazed out at the black sky, the brilliant moon and stars of the tropics.

She turned and said over her shoulder, "I thought something interesting would happen when Captain Redding had to stop at Muscat to pick up the Governor's cousin. This is the infamous Barbary Coast, is it not?"

Miss Trimmer set her novel aside. "Something interesting *did* happen. The Governor's wretched cousin insists he must be delivered to Sharjah. That takes us right through the Straits of Hormuz. That is where the pirates strike you must know, at the narrow entrance to the Persian Gulf. We must have passed through by now. Safely, thank God."

A movement at the edge of her eye caught Lady Melora's attention and she turned back to the window. "There's a ship approaching, Trimmer!" she called excitedly. "One of those dhows—no, two. How pretty they look, with the sails catching the wind. There's another—a whole *fleet* of them.

What can it be? A safe convoy for us, perhaps?''

A look of alarm flitted across Miss Trimmer's
dour face as she hauled herself from the sofa to
view this ominous sight. "Pirates," she breathed,
and clutched her charge's arm for support.

"More likely fishermen," Lady Melora replied,
with a shrug of disappointment.

As they watched, the boats drew closer,
skimming swiftly over the water. The corridor
beyond their cabin was suddenly alive with activity.
Pounding feet and raised voices told them some
unwonted thing was afoot. The ladies exchanged a
frightened glance. There was a loud knock, and
immediately the door was flung open unceremoniously.

"Better lock up ladies," a seaman warned.
"Pirates sighted to starboard."

The blood drained from Miss Trimmer's face.
Even Melora, who had been decrying the lack of
excitement, paled visibly. "Pirates! Oh my God!"
she whispered.

"Into the bedroom and under the bed," Miss
Trimmer said, and began to make haste in the
proper direction, snatching up her valuables as she
ran. "My novel, the tea cannister," she said, quite
at random.

"Our reticules and jewelry," Melora added,
following after her. They bumped into each other
as they flew around the small bedroom, where their
trunks occupied most of the floor space. Melora
cast a forlorn glance at the array of gowns in her
open trunk, some of them never worn.

"You must make yourself ugly, my dear," Miss
Trimmer exclaimed, as it occurred to her what
other booty the pirates might have in mind.

"Thank goodness they won't be wanting *that* sort of thing of me. A *pelisse!* Put something over your body to hide—" It was clear at a glance Lady Melora must be hidden from head to toe. "Everything," she finished in confusion, and threw a cloak over her charge.

The commotion in the corridor ceased; a sudden silence fell like a pall over the cabin. "What's happening?" Miss Trimmer demanded.

Melora struggled out from under the cloak and threw it aside. "Let's go back to the window," she said, and darted into the other room.

By the light of the crescent moon, she had a narrow view of the attack through her cabin porthole. The dhows converged ominously in a semicircle around the frigate, ten of them in all. The silence was broken only by the hish of water against the hull, and the creaking of the rigging.

Aboveboard, Captain Redding had hastened to the helm and held a telescope to his sharp eye. Above him the white sails billowed, occasionally revealing the movement of sailors as they moved about the ropes. The light at the binnacle shone on the weathered visage of the steerman, looking to his Captain for orders.

"We'll never outrun them," Captain Redding said. "Those dhows are light and maneuverable."

"They just popped up from nowhere," the steersman volunteered.

"The coast is lined with creeks running between the mountains. The pirates know every curve and every inlet for hiding. They come and go like phantoms in those light dhows. And us with ladies aboard, and our demmed orders—made up by civilians—forbidding us from shooting first." As he spoke, a volley of fire came at the ship broad-side. A wide smile split Redding's swarthy face. "They're for it now, mate," he exclaimed. "Steady as you go." Then he hastened off to oversee the shooting.

The peaceful moon shone unconcerned from its lofty height, revealing the grizzly battle below. The dhows continued advancing and shooting, drawing the half-circle more tightly around the frigate. Balls of fire hurtled through the blackness, accompanied by an intermittent roar like thunder from the guns. The stern of one dhow was ablaze. From her porthole, Melóra saw a pirate leaping clear of the flames.

As she stood with her heart beating in her throat, there was a wrenching crack, and the room shuddered around her. "We're hit, Trimmer!" she exclaimed.

"Hartshorn! Where's the hartshorn?" Trimmer demanded, and ran to look for it in the teapot.

Melora remained transfixed at the window. The pirates were close enough that, between volleys, bloodthirsty human shouts were heard echoing across the black water. A grappling hook was thrown across on a rope. One dhow pulled itself alongside the Reliant. A plank was thrown across and the first surge of pirates boarded, brandishing swords and pistols. They were met by the grim-faced and determined British sailors.

Miss Trimmer ran back to the window. "We must hide," she gasped. "Quick, Melora, under the bed."

Melora stared at her from eyes dark with fear, but her chin rose in that bold way that Miss Trimmer knew meant trouble. "I will not crawl under the bed and hide like a mouse. If I'm to be taken, I'll go like a lady. They wouldn't *dare* molest me," she said, but her shaking voice betrayed her.

"Ho, would they not! After they've had their way with you, they'll draw and quarter you, and relish it the more for your being a fine lady."

Lady Melora bit her lip and stood undecided a moment. "They'll sink the ship after they take it. We'll both be drowned. I'm going up on deck—I'll jump overboard if necessary," she said, and took one long stride toward the door.

Miss Trimmer pitched her gaunt body against the door with her arms spread. "Not one step beyond this room! You don't know how to swim."

Frustrated, Melora whirled back to the window. In a moment she called to Miss Trimmer, who still stood plastered against the door, too petrified to move. "There's another frigate coming up from behind! It's one of ours, I think. *It is!* It's flying the Union Jack!" she called jubilantly.

Assailed on both sides, the attacking dhows began to sheer off toward the towering cliffs and soon vanished like shadows. The rescue ship gave chase but was too large to follow the smaller crafts into the creeks.

"Now I'm going on deck," Melora said, and pushed past Miss Trimmer, just as Captain Redding came below to see to the ladies' safety.

"Are they gone, Captain?" Miss Trimmer asked fearfully.

"They've scuttled off. Thank God you ladies are safe. I'm afraid we've got a hole in our side. We'll limp to the closest port for repairs. The other frigate—it looked like Leitrim's ship to me—will certainly come back to see if we need help.''

As he spoke, a seaman came along the corridor, pushing half a dozen pirate captives before him, and stopped at the open door to get orders from his Captain.

"Do you want this lot in the hold?" he asked.

"Take them below. I'll quiz them later, if any of them speak English. Leitrim talks their lingo in any case. He might get something out of them.''

Melora looked over his shoulder to see at close range what a pirate looked like. She could almost feel sorry for the bedraggled specimens of humanity that stood huddled at gun point. These were no dashing bandits in kerchiefs and eye patches. Their dark, thin faces looked hungry, and their eyes were black. One man cowered at the rear, hanging his head. She leaned aside to see him, thinking he was hardly more than a boy. His face was paler than the others. His features too lacked the sharpness of the Arabs'. Fear was written large on his youthful countenance. Why he's English, she thought—or European at least. How on earth did he get here? The young man noticed he was being examined and shifted to conceal himself.

When Melora drew her attention back to the conversation, Captain Redding was saying, "Just lock your door, ladies, and I'll return when Leitrim's ship comes back. If we're in any danger of sinking, he'll take you aboard.''

He left, and Trimmer swiftly drew the bolt. "Well," she said grimly, "I hope this has satisfied your craving for excitement, Miss. You must be careful what you ask for, you see, or you might get it. A husband to protect you, that is what you need.''

"What do I need a husband for? Haven't I got *you*?"

"Aye, but a bird in the bush is—" Melora looked expectantly for what foolishness would come next. "Oh, you know perfectly well what I mean."

Melora stretched her arms and smiled exultantly. "What a story to tell when we get home!" she said, and poured a cup of stone cold tea. "Attacked by pirates, Trimmer! I wouldn't have missed it for anything. They looked rather pathetic, don't you think? One of the ship's officers told me the more barren the coast, the more pirates there are. It's the only way they can survive. It's considered quite an honorable profession hereabouts—like smuggling at home."

"There is a vast difference. Smuggling is not stealing, except from the government, and that doesn't count."

"This was much more interesting than having spent two years in India. We shall be quite unique when we get home."

"That will suit you right down to the heels. Rare birds indeed, if we ever *make* it home. There's many a slip 'twixt the cup and the ship."

"Oh, we shall make it. I'm blessed. Did you notice the prisoner at the back of the throng, Trimmer? I'm sure he was European. I wonder what story he has to tell. Probably an orphan left behind when missionaries died or something of that sort. Quite like one of your horrid novels. I mean to ask the Captain's permission to speak to him. In fact, I shall ask mercy for the boy. Send him back home where he belongs. Or perhaps I shall make him a footman," she said pensively.

"Oh, excellent! A pirate for a footman. That will cause a stir indeed in the polite salons of London. The baggage will run off with your jewelry. *I* didn't notice any European. They looked a proper parcel of thieves to me."

"No, one of them was white."

Miss Trimmer noticed her charge was wool gathering, and called her to attention. "Did Captain Redding say Leitrim?"

"I beg your pardon?"

"He said the ship that rescued us was captained by Leitrim. Do you suppose it could be Lord Drumcliff's son?"

"'Who the devil is Lord Drumcliff?"

"An Anglo-Irish earl. And you should not say 'the devil,' my dear. It is uncommonly common. His eldest son is Viscount Leitrim. I do believe Lietrim went to India to pass the time till he inherits his full title and estates. So restless, the Irish lads. I wager it is the same Leitrim."

Melora looked up with the dawning of interest. "Is he single?" she asked.

"I never heard of his having made a match. Certainly one would have heard."

"Handsome?"

"All the Drumcliff clan are handsome. Very well to grass too. They have enormous estates in Country Leitrim. Unfortunately, they are all scoundrels with the ladies."

A mischievous smile lurked at the corners of Melora's lips. "Pity," she said demurely.

Her chaperone tossed up her hands in vexation. "I must have been mad to agree to accompany you to Bombay. The Lord knows I have *tried* to inculcate some notions of propriety into your head.

You can lead a horse to drink, but you cannot—"
Melora waited, smiling. "If it had not been that
your Uncle Harold was Governor there, and in
such wretched health, I would not have considered
it."

"Come now, Trimmer. I wasn't the one who
wanted to go to Bombay in the first place. I wanted
to be presented at Court."

"You were too young and shatter-brained, and
not wealthy enough then to nab a good *parti*."

"I know perfectly well you took me to Bombay
so Uncle Harold would meet me, and hopefully
leave me his fortune when he died. He did, so you
have done your good deed. You and I are well set
for life."

There was another tap at their cabin door and a
junior ship's officer was admitted.

"The Cap'n said to tell you ladies you'd be
changing to Captain Cavan's ship. You might want
to pack up your trunks. Our stern's sporting a hole
as big as your head. We're shipping heavy."

Miss Trimmer's eyes grew and she asked in a
hollow voice, "Are we sinking?"

"Nay, Miss. We'll limp to shore right enough,
but in case we don't make it—"

"We shall begin packing at once. Thank you,
Officer," Lady Melora said crisply. Then she
turned to her chaperone. "We'll have to do it ourselves. *Now* you see I was right in wanting to bring
my *ayah* back with us."

"What we do not need at this time is your old
Indian maid, bawling her head off. My tea cannister, Melora. Don't forget it. I shall have a cup
of tea as soon as we reach *terra firma*."

They began packing up their belongings,

chatting as they worked. "I thought it was Lord Leitrim who was to take us aboard," Melora mentioned. "The officer said Captain Cavan."

"Cavan is the family name of Lord Drumcliff. I was correct in thinking Leitrim is the old earl's son. I wonder where he will take us. Surely to God they don't expect us to camp with Arabs till another ship to England passes by."

"I have no idea," Melora replied, but her tone held no concern. A smile of anticipation lifted her lips as she began putting her toilet articles into a leather traveling case. "We might get to ride a camel, Trimmer, and live in a tent."

Miss Trimmer groaned and clutched her tea cannister to her bosom for consolation.

Chapter Two

It was more than an hour before a knock came at the cabin door to summon the ladies. Miss Trimmer had fallen into a fitful doze, but Lady Melora hopped up with alacrity. Even as she greeted Captain Redding, her eyes slid over his shoulder to examine his companion. She had been envisaging a naval hero akin to Admiral Nelson, decked out in formal attire, tricorne hat trimmed in gold, navy cutaway coat plastered with ribbons and medals. Her spirits sank as she beheld a sailor in a dusty jacket, his white shirtfront torn nearly in two, grimed with gunpowder and splashed with blood that had darkened to brown. A shock of black hair fell over his forehead, and his expression was grim. His dark eyes surveyed her with no sign of pleasure.

"Lady Melora," he bowed stiffly when Captain Redding made the introduction.

"Captain Cavan," she curtsied, equally stiff. It was the name Redding used to introduce him.

"If you're ready, we'll depart immediately," Leitrim said.

"Very well, if you'll just send some men to remove our trunks," she replied.

"Trunks?" Lietrim asked, turning a disgruntled face to Redding. "We can't get half a dozen trunks in the little dhow I captured. It will be crowded with our wounded men and the prisoners."

"I thought we were going in your ship," Melora said.

"It's on patrol duty, under my First Officer. I have some business ashore."

Miss Trimmer roused up at the sound of voices and asked, "Where are you taking us?" Melora also listened to hear the answer.

"To the closest port," Leitrim replied.

"Is there a good hotel there?"

"I hadn't heard the Pulteney opened a branch," Leitrim said ironically. "I know a friendly *shaikh* who'll give you rack and manger till we can get you on to another ship."

"A *shaikh*?" Miss Trimmer exclaimed wildly. "No, no. We do not wish to stay with foreigners!"

"Then you shouldn't have left England," Leitrim growled. "You will find no English drawing rooms in Arabia, Madam. If you prefer to be set ashore to shift for yourself, you might have the good fortune to meet a bunch of non-hostile nomads. I believe you will be more comfortable in a castle than roaming the deserts on a camel's back, sleeping in a tent."

"Quite, quite," Captain Redding said encouragingly. "It will only be for a short time, ladies."

"I suppose beggars can't be losers," Trimmer said forgivingly, and frowned at this untruth.

"That will be fine, Captain," Melora said, addressing herself to Leitrim. She held her head high and stared at him coldly. She wasn't accustomed to being spoken to in this toplofty manner. Then she turned to her chaperone. "A *shaikh* and a castle sound fairly amusing, Miss Trimmer. We shall ask the *shaikh* to show us his harem. Perhaps his girls will teach us to dance, so that we may repay his hospitality."

Leitrim's face stiffened contemptuously. "You have your notions of Arabia from literature. You will find no *hareem*, Lady Melora. Don't go fancying yourself a Scheherazade. Shaikh Rashid is not one of your tame English flirts, to be toyed with."

Her chin rose higher. "Oh I have no use for tame gentlemen, Captain. I always prefer a touch of danger in my flirtations." She turned from him with an exaggerated gesture and spoke to Redding. "Before we leave, Captain, I have a small favor to ask. The prisoners—I should like to see them, if you please."

"I'm afraid that's impossible," the Captain said reprovingly. "I couldn't take a lady into the hold."

"I wasn't suggesting you do so. Could the prisoners not be brought up here?"

"Too dangerous. One of 'em's hopped overboard already."

"It's actually only one I want to see. There was a European amongst them—quite a young man. I should like to speak to him."

"There's no European," Captain Leitrim said firmly. "I've already questioned them."

"I saw a European—he looked English," Melora insisted.

"An hallucination, no doubt, brought on by the fear of the attack," Leitrim said aside to Redding.

"I was not afraid! I'm not a coward. I survived the monsoons of India! I saw a white-faced young man."

"Perhaps he's the one who got away," Redding suggested.

"Very likely," Leitrim agreed, but his eyes still said she was hallucinating. "And now it is high time *we* got away. My first mate will accompany you to Sharjah for repairs, Captain Redding. You'll want to drop the Governor's cousin off there. I'll see the ladies safely ashore and meet you there tomorrow."

"My tea cannister. I cannot leave without my tea," Miss Trimmer said, and looked about for the precious cargo.

Lady Melora snatched up the closest bandbox and followed the stiff-backed Captain Leitrim up on deck. She gritted her teeth and uttered not a word of complaint when he pointed out the means of descent. The ropes used for taking cargo aboard were to be her staircase.

"You first, Lady Melora," he said, with grim satisfaction. "Come now, you're no coward," he taunted. "You must show Miss Trimmer the way. I fear she is entertaining some unladylike idea of arguing."

The water and the dhow awaiting her looked very far away. All around the black water gleamed expectantly, as though waiting to swallow her up. In the pale moonlight, men sat huddled together in the small boat. Some of the wounded were moaning.

Miss Trimmer looked over the railing and said in a quavering voice, "Perhaps we should just stay put."

"Suit yourself," Leitrim said nonchalantly. "The ship *might* get to shore without sinking. I trust you ladies are good strong swimmers?"

The ladies, who had never been in any body of water larger than their bath tub, exchanged a silent, speaking look. "I'll go first," Melora said and steeled herself for the venture.

"This way," Leitrim said, and began attaching the ropes around her.

Melora swayed perilously in the wind as she was let down into the dhow. Every instinct urged her to scream, till she looked up and saw Leitrim's hateful face staring down at her. She gritted her teeth and remained silent. As the rope approached the smaller boat, her heart left her throat and returned to its proper place in her chest. Once safely aboard, she detached the rope and chose a seat to wait for Miss Trimmer's descent. The older woman was trembling and incoherent by the time her feet touched deck. "I felt like a ham hung on the hook to cure," she babbled. "And the swaying. My dear, I really think I shall swoon."

Melora busied herself settling Trimmer down. When she glanced up again, Leitrim was descending by the rope. He hadn't bothered being tied into the seat, but stood with one foot secured in a knot, holding on by only one hand. In the other hand he held Melora's forgotten bandbox. His insouciant smile annoyed her inordinately. She felt he was purposely making the rope sway, to show his bravery, and looked away.

"Thank you," she said tersely when he landed and presented her bandbox with an exaggerated bow. "I hope my hartshorn is in that box."

"If it is, perhaps you'd be kind enough to administer some to my wounded men. You might make yourself useful during the remainder of the trip. I'll scare up a bottle of rum—it'll do them more good than hartshorn."

He strode away, and Miss Trimmer turned a fulminating eye to her charge. "If this cutthroat batch of sailors are fed rum, Melora, we would be safer in the sea with the sharks."

"He won't give them much. Can I leave you alone? You won't have hysterics, or swoon? Here, take the hartshorn," she said, handing Trimmer the bottle. "I shouldn't like to satisfy Leitrim by any show of weakness."

"Just show me to a seat," Miss Trimmer murmured, and sank down on the closest bench.

A seaman brought a keg of rum forward. Melora filled a bottle from the spout and went warily amidst the wounded crew, speaking a few words of encouragement. "Is your arm very sore?" she asked one, who had blood running from his sleeve.

"Don't you worry, Missie. 'Tis only a wee scratch. I'll be back on my pegs in jig time. I couldn't let my ship go to sea without me. I've been with Cap'n these two years. He's a grand officer. He is."

"A hard man but a fair one," another added.

"You've got to be hard at sea. It's a tough life."

Little real help could be administered, but Melora bound up one wounded wrist with her handkerchief and put her pelisse over a sailor who was more seriously wounded.

As they skimmed over the water, she kept a sharp eye out for returning pirates. Vision was limited toward the low wall of mountains on the right, but all seemed quiet and peaceful. After an hour the men had settled into sleep, and she wandered toward the bow. Leitrim stood looking into the distance. Her kid slippers made little sound as she approached. The wind swept his dark hair back, revealing a high brow, a straight nose and rugged jaw. Some trace of the hero hung about him, yet there was a sensitive quality around his lips.

"I thought you'd be at the helm," Melora said.

He turned, startled. The former arrogant impatience had vanished, to be replaced by a softer expression. "One of my men has taken it. Is all quiet aft?"

"Yes."

Leitrim studied the pale face beside him, and noticed it wore a milder look than before. "Sorry if I spoke sharply earlier on. I'm in a hurry to get my men to an infirmary. I fear old Tom Jackson might not make it."

"One of them seems badly hurt. I gave him my pelisse."

"Are you cold?" he asked, and reached instinctively to remove his jacket.

"No! Not at all. The breeze is fair. Is there a hospital nearby?"

"Not a real one, but there's an infirmary at the

shipyard. We'll stop there first, then go to the castle."

"The *shaikh's* castle?"

"Yes, Shaikh Rashid-al-Qasimi's place."

"Are the Arabs on good terms with the English then?"

Leitrim stared. "Good God, no! The tribes are in the midst of religious wars amongst themselves and against us. We're being bitten to death by pirates. We're trying to arrange a truce. The East India Company had one with Sultan bin Suggurd, but that's a dead letter now. We're working on one with Shaikh Rashid. That's why it is important you do nothing to offend him."

"Who is working on this truce?"

"I am representing the East India Company, but on behalf of England. I'm with the Bombay Marines, the E.I.C. Navy. Less gloriously known as the Bombay Buccaneers. Our aim is to ensure safe shipping from India to England. France has managed a treaty with Persia, and with Napoleon at such pains to prevent us—" He hunched his shoulders. "I shouldn't be surprised if the French are behind half this piracy business. But you should be safe enough at the castle."

"When do you think we might continue to England?"

"The sooner the better. There'll be another company cruiser along in a month. It won't be coming into the gulf, but we could ferry you out to meet it. That would probably be best," he said, frowning.

"But would we get through the Straits of Hormuz without being attacked again?" she asked.

"They usually lay off for a while after a thorough trouncing."

"They weren't really trounced tonight—just one dhow taken."

"Quite a few of them shot up though. In any case, they don't leave the gulf, and they won't bother attacking my patrol ship. They know I'm not carrying any valuable cargo. It was Redding's having to bring the Governor's cousin to Sharjah that caused this fracas tonight."

"I'm afraid we're all causing a great deal of bother."

He smiled forgivingly. "Civilians usually do, when they find themselves caught up in war doings. How do you come to be here?"

"I was visiting my uncle, Sir Harold Worth—the Governor of Bombay. It's odd we never met before."

"Yes, I knew Sir Harold slightly. I spend most of my time aboard ship, however. During my leave, I traveled to other parts of the country. Travel is broadening, folks say. And why are you returning home now? Marriage?" he ventured.

"My uncle died a year ago. We had to settle up our affairs in India before returning home."

"You'll be making your curtsey at St. James's in the spring, I should think?"

"Yes."

He studied her, smiling. "You shouldn't have any trouble nabbing a title. I understand you're Sir Harold's heiress."

"I already have a title, Lord Leitrim."

His eyes widened a fraction. "And realize *I* have one as well! You're well informed."

"My chaperone is acquainted with your papa, I

believe. What brought you to India?''

Leitrim looked into the distance. "Boredom. When I left, my father was still a vital, active man. I had no taste for sitting on my thumbs, waiting to take over the reins of the Hall. Better to store up some memories for my dotage. My father's ailing now, however. My three-year stint is over. I shall be returning as soon as I finish up a little business here. I look forward to going home, but I enjoyed the adventure. One meets such interesting ladies abroad,'' he said, with a charming smile. Melora touched her tousled hair in a preening gesture. Leitrim noticed it and added nonchalantly, "A pity it's impossible to see more than their eyes. This *purdah* business—''

The speech that had sounded like a compliment fell to the ground with a thud. "I have been more fortunate in that respect,'' she retaliated. "So thoughtful of the Indians not to hide all those handsome, dusky faces. Is the *shaikh* handsome?'' she asked, as much to annoy him as anything else.

"He might strike a lady that way. I find him rather stiff. Of course you'll have virtually nothing to do with Shaikh Rashid. He'll hold himself aloof from you. The Islam religion urges assistance to unfortunates, but he won't personally welcome you, and of course you won't be meeting anyone else. You shan't leave the castle. Be sure to veil your face if you leave your chamber.''

"Veil my face!'' she exclaimed, highly offended. "I shall do nothing of the sort!''

"When in Rome, Lady Melora. It is the custom of the land.''

"*Purdah* was the custom in India too, but I didn't follow it.''

"There you lived surrounded by the British and were a colony unto yourselves. Here in Arabia you'll be the only young English lady. A naked female face would strike the *shaikh* with the same shock you or I would feel for a naked body. It is not done."

Melora assumed an expression of wide-eyed innocence. "But as I shan't be seeing the *shaikh*, it hardly matters, does it?"

"He may pay a courtesy call, as you are a British guest. You'll have to put a shawl over that gown. Ladies here are more modest about revealing their charms." His eyes skimmed over her gown. The rise of bosoms was visible from his superior height. Three-quarters of her arms were bare, and the material of her gown was light enough to suggest the shape beneath it.

"Do as I say in this matter, milady," he added menacingly. "Critical negotiations are afoot. I'll not have you setting tempers on edge by misbehavior. Try to remember you're a lady."

"And the *shaikh*, I trust, is a gentleman," she replied archly, and walked away.

Leitrim looked after her departing form. That dress revealed more of a woman than Arab eyes were accustomed to seeing. Melora's blonde hair and fair coloring too might excite Shaikh Rashid. The man was no hermit. Leitrim shook his head warily. He sighed, and the frown was transformed to a rakish grin. "Melora," he said softly, trying the name on his tongue as though it were a vintage wine. Then he went to speak to his helmsman.

Chapter Three

Dawn streaked the sky in hues of peach and citron when Lord Leitrim accompanied the ladies ashore. The bedraggled trio dodged around small pools of water trapped in the uneven sand of the beach. The puddles gleamed red in the light of the rising sun. Shaikh Rashid-al-Qasimi's castle was only a short walk away. It rose against the pale sky as they approached, a glowing collection of balconies and ramparts set in the midst of sand and a few straggling palm trees, like something out of The Arabian Nights.

"Cover your faces, ladies," Leitrim ordered.

Through Melora's fatigue, a sprout of defiance shot forth, but she quashed it. "I feel a wreck," she said. "I don't want the *shaikh* to see me looking like this."

She and Miss Trimmer lifted the edge of their pelisses to cover their faces. Leitrim pounded on

24

the huge carved door, and after three or four knocks, the door opened silently inwards. A narrow, swarthy face and a pair of dark, hostile eyes glared out at them. The man was covered from head to toe in a flowing garment. The eyes discovered Leitrim and a smile replaced the glare.

Leitrim spoke to the servant in an unrecognizable language and they were admitted into an empty hallway that stretched into the distance. The floor was covered with patterned tile, and the walls bore intricate inscriptions done in blue and gilt. What struck Melora more strangely than this was the utter lack of furnishings.

"Has the *shaikh* left?" she asked in alarm.

"No, he's sleeping," Leitrim replied. "Salwi will show you to your chambers. I'll call on you this afternoon, after you've rested up. Don't leave your rooms, ladies."

"Where are you going?" Miss Trimmer demanded. "You can't leave us alone!"

"I am to meet Captain Redding at the shipyard. You'll be perfectly safe till I return." He turned to Melora and added firmly, "As long as you remain in your rooms, that is to say. The servants will bring you food."

Melora lowered the tail of her pelisse. Only her eyes were visible, but the angry glitter gave a good indication of her feelings. She turned away and followed the servant up the winding staircase.

"Thank you for all your help, Lord Leitrim," Miss Trimmer said, and shook his hand.

"Keep a tight rein on her," he warned.

"You might as well try to chain the wind. But she's dead tired, and won't give me any trouble for a few hours. Come back as soon as you can." Miss

Trimmer peered all around in fright and scampered off after her charge.

"If that hallway is any example, we'll probably have to sleep on the floor," Melora scolded. "You would think a wealthy *shaikh* could afford some furnishings."

Their apartment was a pleasant surprise. Besides a sitting room, they shared a bedchamber. An intricately carved canopied bed of European design graced one corner of the room. Rich gold curtains fell in folds from the frame, and were repeated at the windows. The usual furnishings of dresser, chairs, toilette and desk were present as well. Underfoot, a rich Persian carpet added a further note of luxury. The water pitcher was of a peculiar long-necked sort and highly patterned.

Melora walked to it and handed it to the servant. "Water, please," she said.

He took the pitcher and backed respectfully from the room, bowing and smiling. As soon as he was gone, the ladies dropped the tails of their pelisses and looked at each other.

"If Lord Leitrim thinks I'm going to stay locked up in this room for a month hiding behind a veil, he is insane," Melora said angrily.

"I'd give my left hand for a nice cup of tea," her chaperone answered, and went to a chair in the corner.

"Don't say that! If they hear you, they'll probably chop it off. Not that they'd understand English. And what's keeping that servant with our water? Oh I'm going to bed, Trimmer. I was never so fatigued in my life."

Melora walked wearily to the bed, kicked off her slippers and lay down on top of the counterpane, fully dressed. Miss Trimmer frowned pensively at her soiled gown and perfectly filthy stockings.

"Your rose silk is beyond repair, and all our clothes are on Redding's ship. Perhaps Leitrim will bring them back with him."

She waited to hear Melora's retort. From the bed there was only a slight twitching as Lady Melora fell into a deep, exhausted slumber. Miss Trimmer went to the door and drew the bolt before joining her. "I don't want that ghost sneaking in on us to chop off our arms," she murmured.

It was several hours before the ladies were roused by a loud banging on their door. Melora was the first to stir. She roused Miss Trimmer. "It's probably only the servant with water," she said, and jumped up.

"Cover your face!l" Trimmer called after her.

"Oh bother!" Melora grabbed up a towel from the wash stand and threw it over her head.

She was happy to see the male servant had been replaced by a female. The woman wore a long flowing garment and was completely veiled. Her face covering was of a sheer, transluscent black material that permitted her to see, and gave Melora a hazy impression of dark eyes. The woman's manner was extremely modest and deferential. Behind her came a whole row of female servants, bearing a tin hip bath, water and soap, perfume, a tray of food, clothes and a large bouquet of flowers. The women—girls really—entered in a row like soldiers, and took possession of the room, whispering and giggling, and staring through their veils with unconcealed curiosity at these pale visitors. It was Melora's blonde hair and blue eyes that particularly engrossed them. They had never seen anything like it.

"Ayesha," the leader said quietly, and pointed at herself. Her movements were graceful as she directed the girls.

"Ayesha—that must be her name," Miss Trimmer said.

As the servants arranged their burdens about the room, Melora examined them. These must be a special retinue of the *shaikh's* personal servants. The girls were modestly but richly dressed. Some wore pretty open sandals, others a strange sort of bootee that turned up at the toe. Gold bracelets tinkled as they went about their duties. One was pouring coffee, another pouring water into the basin, another laying out the rich silk materials, all under the watchful eye of Ayesha, who was obviously in charge of them. Melora observed that this oriental garb could be very attractive.

When the bath was poured, Ayesha looked expectantly at Lady Melora, and pointed at the tub.

"They surely don't expect us to unrobe in front of them!" Miss Trimmer gasped.

"Yes Lady," Ayesha said encouragingly.

"She speaks English!" Melora exclaimed.

"Ask her for tea," Miss Trimmer said at once.

Ayesha spoke to one of the girls and a small cup of jet black coffee was handed to Miss Trimmer. She was led firmly to the chair.

Two other servants held a sheet in front of Melora and began to undress her. "They're only girls," Melora said apologetically to her chaperone. Then she slid into the hip bath and emitted a sigh of pure luxury as the warm water closed over her. She was scrubbed with scented soap till her body tingled.

"Enough," she said at last, and stood up.

A pitcher of clean water was poured over her, a sheet wrapped around her, and she was led to the silk gown, that had no discernable form. It was a pale rose, similar in color to the gown cast aside on the floor. The beautiful shawl that accompanied it was multicolored, an intricate pattern with much gold interwoven. When it was on, she slid her toes into a pair of gilt sandals and went to make a playful curtsey before Miss Trimmer.

"Shameful!" Trimmer scolded. "You can practically see through that material."

"Then I shan't have to damp it, as the ladies are doing in London this season," Melora said pertly. She glided to the mirror and examined herself. "I think it's pretty. I shall see if the *shaikh* wants to give it to me as a present. I'll wear it at my first masquerade party when we get home, Trimmer, and set a new style. See if I don't. We shall be all the crack, hot from the orient, with tales of pirates and *shaikhs* to add lustre to our reputation."

Ayesha turned and stared at the word "*shaikh*." She silently handed Melora the head veil, which Melora cast aside with a smile. Ayesha handed it to her again, and again it was discarded.

"Don't be asking him for anything," Trimmer warned. "You don't get a gift for nothing, my girl."

"I thought that was the very essence of a gift. Your turn for the bath, Trimmer. Ayesha is having the tub emptied."

"I shall bathe myself, thank you. But not till I

have had breakfast. This coffee is impotable—thick as gravy. It would keep an insomniac awake.''

"You don't want to sleep again so soon, do you?'' Melora laughed. "That fruit looks delicious,'' she added, and took up a bunch of green grapes. Sweet cakes accompanied the meal. "I never had honeyed sweets for breakfast before. Actually they're quite good.

"I should prefer gammon and eggs.''

"When in Rome, Trimmer.''

Melora looked about the busy room and smiled. "This might not be so bad,'' she said pensively. "I can hack it for a month.''

"What is that dreadful scent they've doused you in?''

Melora lifted her wrist and sniffed daintily. "Jasmine, I think. The *shaikh* certainly has a great many servants.''

"Aye, every one of them pretty young gels. That gives you an idea what sort of man he is.''

"The sort who likes pretty girls? He sounds almost English.''

"It won't do to be too free with him, if he happens to grant us an audience. Remember what Leitrim said.''

"The devil with Leitrim. I'm sick of hearing his name.''

The servants were just beginning to urge Miss Trimmer toward the fresh bath water when there was a knock on the door.

"The *shaikh*!'' Melora exclaimed. Her heart pounded, and two splashes of pink stained her cheeks.

"Our veils!''

They both snatched up their dainty veils and attached them awkwardly. When they were in place, Lady Melora called, "Ayesha!", and pointed to the door.

Ayesha glided forward and opened it, revealing not the *shaikh* but Lord Leitrim. Melora stared in surprise at what came next. Ayesha nearly leapt in alarm. What was the matter with the woman? Had she never seen a white man before? And why was Leitrim making his prettiest bow to a mere servant? Ayesha clapped her hands; the girls quickly gathered up their equipment and darted out as though frightened for their very lives.

After Leitrim had lost his chance of being a hero, Melora was annoyed that he now chose to come looking like one. All the finery of a naval captain's uniform and an impressive array of medals won him only a scowl.

"Oh, it's only you," she said, and dropped her veil.

"Sorry I couldn't be Lord Byron. He would appreciate your getup." That was his only acknowledgment that she wore a completely new and rather becoming style. "I see you've met Ayesha."

"We had some hopes she might speak English, but 'Yes, lady' appears to be her sole vocabulary," Trimmer explained, with a sorry glance at her coffee cup.

"That's safer than only knowing how to say, 'Yes, gentleman,' " Melora smiled impishly.

Leitrim's nostrils pinched in distaste. "It is a blessing Ayesha couldn't understand your conversation, if this is the way you carry on."

"Is she your flirt, Leitrim?" Melora asked knowingly. "It's obvious we tread on your toes by

making sport of her. I believe it's high time Lord
Leitrim went home, Trimmer, before he makes a
misalliance with a serving wench."

"It may interest you to know Ayesha is the
shaikh's sister. She has done you the honor of
letting you use her personal servants, and this is
your notion of gratitude! You would both be set
loose in the desert without water if Shaikh Rashid
had any notion of what you're saying. Women here
are held in the highest esteem, and kept isolated
from men. Even *you* must have noticed her alarm
at finding me at the door."

"Yes, even we, insensitive though we are to
propriety, couldn't fail to notice she jumped like a
gaffed salmon at the sight of you," Melora
retorted. "I made sure you had been chasing her
into dark corners, and she was only afraid you
meant to pinch her derrière."

Leitrim's face worked with the effort to restrain
his temper. "I know how to behave with a real
lady. I am not even permitted to meet her, except in
her brother's presence. You may be sure there is no
pinching going forth."

"You mustn't think of it, Leitrim!" Trimmer
warned. "They'll cut off your hand. It isn't worth
it."

Leitrim looked at her as though she were a
Bedlamite. Melora said, "Perhaps Lord Leitrim
thinks it *is* worth it, Miss Trimmer. I believe we
have stumbled across a blocked romance here."

"If you ever say anything of the sort within the
shaikh's hearing, I will box your ears."

"Then your boast that you know to behave with
a lady is false, milord."

"I said a *real* lady."

Melora's eyes flashed. "As opposed to my spurious title, you mean, that has only been in the family for three hundred years? The Worths were noblemen when the Leitrims were cutting peat in the bogs of Ireland."

"I'm not quite such a parvenu as that. As to three hundred years of nobility, I should think by now some manners would have been bred into you."

"Well, you think wrong," Trimmer assured him. "I have been trying for three years myself, but she is incorrigible."

"Then I shall make an excuse to Shaikh Rashid," Leitrim decided. "He had asked if he might come to meet you, but obviously we can't let him hear this hoyden. *He* understands English," Leitrim said, and turned to stride angrily from the room.

"Wait!" Melora shouted, and ran after him, grabbing his arm. "I'm sorry, Leitrim. I was only teasing," she said, and smiled demurely. "If I had had any notion Ayesha was his sister, I wouldn't have said anything. It was only my wretched temper."

Leitrim looked at her fingers, clutching his arm. He looked at her conning smile, and felt his anger dissipate. "Well, Shaikh Rashid did want to meet you, and it would be awkward to make excuses. But for God's sake, hold that wretched tongue of yours, Lady Melora. Act the way Ayesha acted. Shy, modest."

She put on her veil, lowered her head and held her hands folded in front of her.

"You're not going to be canonized, only introduced," Leitrim laughed.

"Thank God for that!" Trimmer exclaimed. "It would be exceedingly uncomfortable to have your arm shot off, Melora." Melora dropped her veil and exchanged a laughing look with Leitrim.

"You'd best keep your tongue between your teeth too, Miss Trimmer," he said.

"You may be sure I shall."

"I'll bring him up right away then, if you're ready, ladies?"

"I look a perfect dowd!" Miss Trimmer said, looking at her dusty gown.

"I have an uncomfortable feeling it's Lady Melora he wants to see." With a frown, Lietrim left the room, and Melora smiled contentedly.

Chapter Four

It was a few moments before the expected knock on the door was heard. Miss Trimmer went haltingly forward to open it. Melora gazed, and knew she was looking at the *shaikh*. That arrogant stare and proudly held body could only belong to a ruler. He wore a pristine white *burnous* of flowing silk. Around his head, a twisted gold band held it in place. His bronzed complexion contrasted dramatically with all the white. Eyes like hot black coffee deigned to seek out his English guests. They skimmed lightly over Trimmer and settled on Melora.

Leitrim stepped forward and made introductions. "Your Excellency, permit me to present Lady Melora Worth, and her companion, Miss Trimmer."

The ladies curtsied; the *shaikh* regarded them stolidly. He did not smile, nor offer them his hand, nor bow. "Welcome to my home," he said. "I am honored to entertain you, ladies." But his tone, his manner, indicated that the honor was all theirs. "Ayesha," he said, and looked behind him.

His sister, unseen till that moment, drifted out from behind him and nodded her head. "This is my sister, Ayesha," the *shaikh* said. "She makes her home with me since the death of her husband. Unfortunately, she speaks no English."

The English ladies nodded at her. Ayesha remained motionless, staring from behind her diaphanous veil.

"Lord Leitrim will attend to your needs," the *shaikh* announced. "Good day, ladies."

With a sort of abbreviated bob of his head, he turned and swept away in a cloud of white silk. His sister followed in his wake, like a cygnet gliding over a pond after the mother swan. Leitrim remained behind.

"Well, that didn't go too badly," he said.

The ladies put off their bothersome veils. "So that was the great Shaikh Rashid-al-Qasimi," Trimmer said. "Not exactly a chatterbox, is he?"

"Oh but did you see his *eyes*, Trimmer!" Melora sighed. "How handsome! And romantic!"

"He reminded me of the gypsies who mend pots at home, and steal chickens. Ha, she had an eye for one of *them* too," Trimmer added aside to Leitrim.

Relieved that the meeting had passed without incident, Leitrim was in a good mood. "A pity she couldn't try her charms on Shaikh Rashid, but you see now how he behaves. Very stiff and proper. I must be off, ladies."

"You'll get our trunks from Captain Redding?" Trimmer reminded him. Melora wasn't listening. She stood bemused, thinking of the handsome *shaikh*.

"It will be best if you wear oriental outfits while you're here. They're more concealing."

That Melora put up no argument was a good indication of her state. Leitrim left, giving Melora a good opportunity to tire Trimmer's ears with rapturous outpourings about the *shaikh*. As the tedious days wore on, the compliments petered out to complaints.

"Three days we've been locked up in this room, Trimmer! And the *shaikh* hasn't even had the courtesy to invite us to join him for dinner. Honored to entertain us indeed! Is this his notion of entertainment?"

"It is peaceful," Trimmer pointed out, taking a break from the vigorous wielding of her fan. "Onc could not be very active in this warm climate."

"It's bloody hot."

"Ladies are never hot, my dear. We are only permitted to be warm, no matter if we are baked to a jelly. If only I had brought some novels with me I could endure the warmth. Leitrim brought me some of the *shaikh's* French books, but they, you know, are so terribly hard to understand that I end up with the megrims. Leitrim said we may walk on the balcony and look at the ocean, so long as we are veiled."

"I'm sick to death of looking at the ocean. I hope I never see another ocean. Shaikh Rashid has excellent mounts. Why does he not permit us to ride them?"

"Ha, if beggars were wishes, horses would ride.
And you forget we have Leitrim's company in the
evening, as often as he can spare us time."

"Which is too often to suit me!"

"You always seem very happy to see him."

"I'm so bored by nightfall I'd be happy to see a
yahoo. I'm going to write to Cousin Arabella."

"You'll put the poor girl in debtors' prison,
having to pay for so many letters."

Melora went to the desk and took up the quill.
She gazed out the window at the endless expanse of
gleaming ocean, sighed wearily, and wrote. 'Dear
Arabella: I only have time for a quick note. Shaikh
Rashid keeps us so well entertained here. Did I tell
you he has a stable of Arabian blood horses? And a
yacht, of course, and he raises falcons. We have
not had time yet to try our hand at falconry.'

She was interrupted by Leitrim's knock on the
door. She dropped the quill and hastily shoved her
letter into the drawer.

Passing in the hall an hour later, Shaikh Rashid
heard the sound of laughter from the ladies' apartment. It was an alien sound to his ears, the silvery
and unrestrained tinkle of feminine laughter. How
boldly outspoken the English ladies were! They
showed a very poor respect for their gentlemen. He
stood a moment listening, intrigued. His face wore
a wistful expression as he walked on alone to his
private apartment.

He asked to have Leitrim sent to him when he
was free. In half an hour, Leitrim stood before
him.

"Your Excellency," he bowed.

Shaikh Rashid waved him toward a pillow. "My
guests, they are comfortable, milord?"

"Very comfortable, sir."

"English ladies are not accustomed to such close confinement, I think."

"You have graciously permitted them to take the air along the balcony."

"I regret that my sister does not speak English. She could make their visit more interesting. As this is impossible, I have decided to invite Lady Melora to my apartment for coffee tomorrow. Her chaperone will accompany her, *ça va sans dire.* And yourself, milord."

"But how can they take coffee in their veils?"

"In England they take coffee with gentlemen—is it not so?"

"Yes, but—"

"What is acceptable behavior for ladies in England will be acceptable to me here."

"That's very gracious of you, sir, but it is entirely unnecessary. The ladies—"

Shaikh Rashid turned a dark, imperious eye on Leitrim. "My decision has been taken, sir. You will inform the ladies."

"Yes, Your Excellency."

Leitrim waited till the next morning to inform them. His grim expression gave no hint of the treat he was about to confer.

"That thundercloud on your brow indicates rain," Melora said. "And very welcome it would be too in this hothouse."

"Is there something amiss?" Trimmer asked.

"On the contrary—I have good news."

"You have word of a ship to take us home?" Miss Trimmer asked hopefully.

"Not yet."

"You've brought our clothes?"

"I'll attend to that as soon as possible. More pressing matters had to be arranged."

"There is no more pressing matter than our gowns, Leitrim," Miss Trimmer assured him. "They will all be a mess of wrinkles. I wonder if the *shaikh* has an iron or any facility to press them."

"Lord Leitrim is referring to the ship and his men," Melora said. "Is everything under control? That badly wounded man—he didn't die?"

"Not yet—I hope he may pull through. They're cobbling up Redding's ship. It may be able to continue on its way before the monthly frigate from Bombay. Perhaps your best chance to get home will be to rejoin it."

"I would offer you a drink, Leitrim," Miss Trimmer said, "but that coffee, I fear, isn't fit for human consumption."

"Actually, I came to invite you to take coffee with the *shaikh*."

Melora gave a convulsive start, and a quick smile of triumph flashed over her face. "That removes the odium of my visit, I notice," he said through thin lips. "You must not take it as a personal compliment, however. He merely wishes to show every courtesy to his English visitors, as an augur of his intention regarding the truce. You will remember what I said about the behavior expected of you, Lady Melora."

"I don't require deportment lessons from a Captain. I have met princes and *nawabs* in India. I know how to conduct myself in polite company."

"It is not the politeness of the company that concerns me, but the cultural differences. In

Arabia, young ladies are seen, not heard.''

She gave him a bold look. "I trust Shaikh Rashid-al-Qasimi will at least like what he sees.''

"What he will see is your veil.''

"Am I permitted to say 'good day' at least, or must I literally act like a deaf-mute throughout the visit?''

Leitrim frowned uncertainly. "The *shaikh* has some familiarity with European manners. He knows our women are raised differently. You may say a few words of thanks for his hospitality.'' He turned to Miss Trimmer. "And an older lady is permitted a certain degree of freedom. You needn't keep your tongue beneath your teeth, Miss Trimmer.''

"I shan't be able to utter a word. I'm trembling like a blancmange. And I am still wearing the gown I arrived in, for I refuse to wrap myself up in a sheet like a corpse. He will think me a dowd.''

Leitrim's dark eyes skimmed over Melora's costume—the same one given to her by Ayesha. "Lady Melora will uphold England's reputation in that field. Very fetching, ma'am. Veils on, ladies. We're off.''

Lord Leitrim led them along echoing corridors, all tiled and arched and decorated with those symbols that resembled hieroglyphics. Servants in *burnouses* scuttled to and fro, staring, full of curiosity.

"I feel like a freak at a raree show," Melora complained.

"Now you know how the bearded lady at Bartholomew Fair feels," Leitrim replied.

"She could shave off her beard if she wanted to.

I can hardly grow a dusky skin."

"And wouldn't if you could, I fancy. You enjoy your unique position. This is it," he said, and drew to a stop before a trellised door.

He tapped deferentially and waited. An elegant male servant dressed in a long *burnous* admitted them. It was another of those strangely empty spaces that the group entered. Were it not for the rich carpets underfoot and the azure sky seen through the windows, the place would have looked bleak. Bleakness was not the word that occurred to Melora. She found it strangely peaceful, particularly as the *shaikh* was not yet present. Tasseled cushions were arranged around a small, low table. As they approached, the table was seen to be highly ornamented. The center was done in tarsia work with mother of pearl and wood, the frame was intricately carved in a pattern of curving leaves. A large book in a gold cover was open on the table, its pages decorated with illustrations around the edges.

Other small tables and low stools stood around the walls of the room, holding Islamic objets d'art. Foreign-looking, but beautiful. The servant glided away, and the three guests stood looking at each other.

"This is strange manners indeed!" Miss Trimmer objected.

"Would you expect the Prince Regent to wait on your pleasure if you were invited to Carlton House?" Leitrim asked. "Shaikh Rashid is the supreme ruler of this domain. And incidentally, if you address him, use the words 'Your Excellency.' He'll be along shortly."

"I'll never get up again if I have to sit on the floor," was Miss Trimmer's next complaint.

"I'll haul you up, Miss Trimmer. If he tells you to sit, you sit. Otherwise remain standing and keep your head bowed."

A motion at the open doorway caught their attention. Melora looked eagerly to see if she had remembered the *shaikh* as he really was, or if imagination had painted him in more romantic hues. It was the same arrogant face and proudly held head. The eyes, perhaps, wore a different expression—was it interest? She noticed that Ayesha had flowed in behind her brother and stood modestly behind him.

Leitrim noticed too, and was surprised at her inclusion in the party. It was the first chance he had had to examine her closely. Thus far he knew her only as a dark figure gliding past in hallways, or glimpsed on a balcony. Without meaning to, he found himself gazing at her through her veil. He had an impression of dark eyes, a tantalizing glimpse of delicate features. For a moment their eyes met and held, then she lowered her head.

The *shaikh* stared with those peculiarly impassive eyes at Melora. When he had satisfied his first curiosity, he spoke. "Please be seated, ladies," he said. His voice was soft as fog, but with a buzz of authority.

Melora looked uncertainly at Leitrim, and performed a curtsey. Miss Trimmer gulped and followed suit. The *shaikh* indicated the pillows with a graceful wave of his hand, and took up the central pillow behind the table himself. Lietrim hopped to Miss Trimmer's side to aid her descent.

When he turned to help Melora, she had seated herself beside the *shaikh*. Already she had broken a rule! She ought to have left the more privileged seat for the man.

He noticed there was coffee on a side table, but the ladies' veils prevented their partaking of it. No indication had been given thus far of how this feat was to be accomplished. Certainly Ayesha would not unveil in front of him. The *shaikh* turned to Lady Melora and said, "My servants have provided all that you require—yes?"

She nodded her head docilely and bit her lip. This is ridiculous, she thought. How can I talk to him if I'm not allowed to speak? Leitrim nodded Miss Trimmer into speech.

"Very kind, Your Excellency. We have been well tended, thank you."

But it was obviously the younger lady's thanks that were wanted. Shaikh Rashid stared at her in unconcealed curiosity, waiting. "Thank you, Your Excellency," she said, in a voice so low it was almost inaudible, but its softness excited him.

"You will tell Leitrim all that you wish," he said. "It is my pleasure to supply your needs."

Again Melora nodded. This time, it was Leitrim who filled the conversational void. "I hope we shan't have to impose on your hospitality too long, Shaikh Rashid."

A gentle smile curved the *shaikh's* lips. "Do not hurry my guests' departure, Lord Leitrim. It is not frequent I have the opportunity to speak with an English lady." As though on a sudden impulse, he turned to his sister and spoke to her in Arabic. She rose silently from her pillow and glided out the door. Leitrim assumed the coffee would be served now.

"I understand you have come from Bombay, Lady Melora," he continued. "You prefer Arabia, yes?"

Wishing to be polite, she nodded silently once more. The *shaikh* put his head back and laughed. White teeth gleamed in his swarthy face. "You are afraid of me! Who gives me such a fierce character? It is Lord Leitrim, I think. I have been told English ladies of high birth make very free in male company."

Leitrim leapt in to explain. "It is true such noblewomen as Lady Melora, whose father is a very highly placed and influential gentleman, mingle with the opposite sex at home. But when we travel, you know—" An impatient glance from the *shaikh* brought him to a halt.

"I wish to hear your voice, milady. Speak, please, to me."

Lady Melora turned a triumphant eye on Leitrim and said, "Well, that's a relief! I was beginning to feel like a toy doll. As you were kind enough to inquire for our comfort, Your Excellency, might I be bold enough to ask for a chair for Miss Trimmer? You can see she is not at all comfortable on the floor."

"Bravo!" the *shaikh* laughed, and clapped his hands. Servants appeared, and a chair was commanded. "You also prefer the chair?" he asked Melora.

"If you prefer the floor, that is quite all right with me. I don't mind."

"Next time, we shall meet in my European

salon. I possess such a chamber, but use it usually only for European gentlemen.''

Leitrim gave a mental moan at that menacing 'next time.' A *bergère* chair was carted in and Lady Trimmer was helped up from the floor. She sank with relief into a proper chair and began massaging her knees.

Again the *shaikh* addressed himself to Melora. ''You must feel free to possess yourself of the castle, and not stay confined in one room.''

Already Leitrim was in a state of anxiety. Melora's next speech sent him reeling with horror.

''May I venture beyond the castle, Your Excellency?'' she asked at once. ''I am not accustomed to being kept within walls. I'm sure your Arabia offers many interesting sights to a traveler.''

The *shaikh* considered her request for a moment. ''A guide shall be placed at your disposal. You will wish to see the mosque, the *souk*—the market place, the desert perhaps from the edge. Do you ride?''

Leitrim made a jerking motion, as though to object, but remained silent.

''I adore riding!'' Melora exclaimed. ''And I have seen your marvelous horses from my balcony.''

The *shaikh* gave a surprised smile. ''I have the best stud farm in all of Arabia. We shall ride one day, when I am free.''

''That would be wonderful! The horses in India were hopeless.''

''I keep only blood Arabian horses. Lord Leitrim will tell you.''

"A very fine stable," Leitrim agreed. "His Excellency is kind enough to lend me a mount when I am visiting. However, all the *shaikh's* mounts are fiery, high-spirited animals. Not suitable for a lady," he said firmly.

"I am an experienced rider," Melora said, with equal firmness. "I have been hunting since I was twelve. When may I ride, sir?"

"It will be arranged at my discretion," the *shaikh* told her imperiously.

She shook her head impatiently. "Yes, but when?" The motion loosened her veil. One corner fell free. She grabbed at it. The *shaikh* reached out a long-fingered hand and removed the veil.

Sapphires was the unoriginal word that popped into his head as he gazed into her wide blue eyes. The blue was deeper than the azure skies of summer, yet not so dark as an angry ocean. It was the heavy fringe of lashes that lent them that deep color. And the skin! Praise be to Allah, the girl had a complexion like fresh rose petals—dipped in Devonshire cream, for her skin was dewy with youth. His black eyes traveled slowly from that tantalizing glint of golden curls showing beneath her shawl, over the rose *burnous*—utterly the wrong color! She must wear blue. Slowly his eyes continued their tour, that could almost be called a sojourn, for the seconds stretched long while he gazed at her with intense interest. Her lips stood out like cherries in that pale, beautiful face.

"You permit?" he asked, but his tone was assertive, and the deed already done. It was only his lambent eyes that held a question.

'A naked female face would strike the *shaikh*

with the same shock you or I would feel for a naked body.' That's how she felt, as though she were stripped naked, with those black eyes burning over her with feverish intensity. A warm flush crept up her neck, coloring her cheeks. This was ridiculous! There was nothing wrong with showing her face. All of England and half of Bombay had already seen it.

"Of course, Your Excellency," she said, trying for an air of nonchalance.

And still he went on staring, as though he'd never seen a woman's face before. She met his gaze, and took the opportunity to study him. What a bold woman it is, the *shaikh* thought. She dares to look me in the eye. I should enjoy to tame this one.

"But only in the privacy of my own personal chambers," the *shaikh* cautioned. "These charms are too precious for the masses. Such rare jewels would only excite their lust and greed. They must be hidden away like my jewels. I shall show you my jewels one day, Lady Melora. But now I see Leitrim is eager to be off. I have matters to discuss with my *khalifah*—religious matters," he added, glancing at the open book before him. "We must discuss religion one day. You will be interested to learn about the Koran. It is to us Muslims what your Bible is to Christians."

On this speech he waved his hand. Leitrim helped Lady Melora up from the pillows. He bowed two or three times; Lady Melora curtsied again, and the three guests left. Before entering the public hallway, Melora affixed her veil.

"How charming the *shaikh* is after all," Melora said.

"He was only being polite to his honored English guests," Leitrim pointed out.

Trimmer's head turned sharply. "Polite? It is a strange way of being polite. He invited us for coffee and didn't give us any. Which is a blessing, for the stuff is undrinkable."

"He was more upset than he let on," Melora said. "His fingers were trembling when he removed my veil."

"I've given him the idea you're a sort of super princess," Leitrim explained.

"I noticed you also resurrected my father from the grave. Why did you do that?"

"It's best to let him think you have a highly placed and influential father still alive. It will inhibit any notions he may be hatching regarding your eligibility."

"I *am* eligible. I have fifty thousand pounds."

"I should have said availability. It wasn't marriage I meant."

They returned to the ladies' chamber and Miss Trimmer turned a wrathful eye on Leitrim. "You aren't suggesting he might try something—"

"His eyes suggested it to me. I don't like this business of ripping off Lady Melora's veil. You remember what I said about how your bare face would affect him," he reminded her.

Melora slowly reached up and removed the veil. With a saucy smile, she dropped it in a waste basket. "You, of course, being a hardened sailor, feel no such shock at my nakedness. I found the *shaikh* most agreeable. I do look forward to riding out with him in the near future."

Chapter Five

Lord Leitrim's quill moved slowly as he sat composing a letter addressed to His Excellency, the Governor of Bombay. "Last week Captain Redding's Reliant was attacked, ostensibly by Joasimee pirates. The dhow we captured, however, contained French guns and ammunition—no Frenchmen aboard. I suspect a certain Monsieur Duval is involved. He masquerades his pirates as Joasimees, knowing Shaikh Rashid is loath to go to war with them. I have seen Duval in company with Rahma b. Jabir, an outlaw Joasimee brigand. The difficulty in proving Duval's involvement is the relative invulnerability of their stronghold at Raz-al—Khaimah. The Joasimees who inhabit it are fierce and hostile to the English. Rahma b. Jabir has enough influence (or money) that he is tolerated there. Access by water is impossible—hundreds of inlets, all well guarded. By land Raz-al-Khaimah is protected by the mountains; the fort there is close to impregnable. I have made contact with a shepherd who pastures his herd in the foothills of the mountains. With his help, I am endeavoring to discover a route into the fort."

Leitrim stuck his quill in his mouth and read what he had just written. "And get my bloody head blown off when I get there," he muttered.

He rose and began pacing the room. Unlike the chamber supplied to the ladies, Leitrim's apartment at the castle was austere. The only concession to European taste was the desk and chair. He glanced through the window and gave such a start he nearly fell out. What was that wretched girl, Melora, doing but walking with the *shaikh!* At least they were chaperoned by Ayesha. He threw on his jacket and darted out the door. Under her curtained veil, he recognized Miss Trimmer, just coming from her room.

She peered through it and said, "Ah, there you are, Leitrim. I was just coming to search you out. The *shaikh* has invited us to tea at four o'clock in his European salon. I dread to think what a botch they will make of tea. I am bringing my own cannister along just in case," she said, and held the red tin up for his perusal.

"When did this happen?"

"I received a note half an hour ago. I thought we would all be more comfortable if you could join us. One appreciates the protection of an English gentleman in foreign lands."

Leitrim was so agitated he didn't bother correcting the lady. Englishman indeed! He was Irish! "What's Lady Melora doing with him?"

"Oh, is he with her?" Miss Trimmer asked,

surprised but not alarmed. "He sent his sister along to show Melora the castle. I was so fagged I lay down for a little rest. No doubt they bumped into the *shaikh* somewhere along the way. He is quite charming, is he not? Very gentlemanly, getting a chair for me—and now inviting us to tea. Melora feels that is to show his respect to me. I am the one who loves tea. Where is his European salon?"

"This way," Leitrim said, and led her along corridors till they reached it.

The salon was as elegant as any drawing room, but what struck the two was that it was empty of people. "They'll be along shortly," Miss Trimmer said, and walked toward a sofa. "Oh look, the *shaikh* has a pianoforte! Melora will be happy to see that. She has been bemoaning the lack of one."

There was the sound of chatter from the hall, and turning, Leitrim saw the party approaching. Ayesha was just gliding away from them, back to her own quarters. He had one glimpse of her veiled face before she lowered her head and departed. He disliked Melora's possessive hand on the *shaikh's* elbow, he disliked that the *shaikh* was smiling, and what he disliked most of all was that Monsieur Henri Duval was with them.

"What's that Frenchmen doing here? Duval must be courting the *shaikh* to scotch the signing of the truce," he said in a low voice.

When they were in the salon, Melora removed her face covering with a sigh of relief.

The *shaikh* made introductions. "You two gentlemen have met, I think?" he said, as Duval and Leitrim shook hands.

"But yes," Duval smiled affably. He was a

dapper man of middle years. His toilette went beyond elegance to proclaim him a dandy. The reek of lavender water issued from him like a fog.

"You're still here, monsieur?" Leitrim asked. "Last time we spoke, you were on the point of leaving. Did you not manage to buy the pearls you were looking for? A *bijou* for Empress Josephine, was it not?"

They all sat down and the conversation continued. "So it was," Duval said, "but now that Josephine has been repudiated, Marie Louise would have been the recipient—if I had managed to procure the pearls, *c'est à dire*. Unfortunately, His Excellency overbid me," Duval added, with a forgiving smile to the *shaikh*.

"Ah, but I let you have the Empress of the Orient, Duval," the *shaikh* reminded him. He turned to Melora and added, "We are discussing only a pearl here, Lady Melora, not a woman. The Empress was an enormous baroque pearl, somewhat rose in color. It was from Ceylon," he added, with a note of disparagement. "The finest pearls come from our Persian Gulf."

The tea tray was brought in and placed before Lady Melora. "You will have the honor of pouring for us," the *shaikh* told her. His dark eyes studied her profile as she lifted the silver pot and the amber liquid steamed into the cup. His gaze continued down her throat and over her body, lingering on her hands, that reminded him of white doves, fluttering gracefully.

"A spoonful of honey," he said. She examined the tea tray and discovered the pot of honey, but no sugar. "For the future, you will know that is how I take my tea," he said. The arrogance of his tone was softened by the glow of admiration in his eyes.

She gave him a long look. "I shall remember that, sir," she answered.

The others added their own milk and honey. Miss Trimmer closed her eyes and drew a long, anticipatory sigh. Then she put the cup to her lips and sipped. Her face screwed up as if she were drinking vinegar. It was all she could do not to spit the dreadful stuff out.

The *skaikh* regarded her in alarm. "It is not good?" he demanded. His mood hovered between surprise and incipient anger. Leitrim gave Trimmer a quelling look.

"It is fine, Your Excellency," she said in a weak voice and set her cup down.

Melora tasted hers and wrinkled her nose in distaste. "It's wretched!" she said bluntly. "The milk is sour."

"Goat's milk," Leitrim explained. "It has a slightly—different taste."

"Then we have another cup, *sans* milk," the *shaikh* decided, and nodded to the servants for fresh tea.

"It is also weak, and not very hot," Melora added. "Trimmer, I see you have your tea cannister. Will you permit me to make the tea for you, sir?"

The *shaikh* considered the request a moment and said with great condescension, "It is permitted—for *you,* mam'selle." He spoke to the servants and snapped his fingers. They bowed obsequiously and disappeared.

"Tea is not our drink," he explained. "We excel

in coffee. It is wise for a country to consume its own resources. In times of war, foreign shipping is interrupted. The English are foolish to rely on foreign tea. They ought to drink—'' He stopped, thinking.

"Milk?" Duval suggested, and laughed. "Not to suggest the anglais are milksops, Lord Leitrim. I see you scowling at me. In France, of course, we have the world's finest wines and brandy."

"We make excellent ale," Lady Melora said, hot to defend her native land. "And gin and whiskey—all sorts of things."

"Ah, gin," Duval shook his head doubtfully. "Blue ruin! It ought to be outlawed. What an insidious drink it is—quite ruining the lower classes."

"Here is the hot water," Trimmer said, and removed the lid from her precious cannister.

"First we must heat the pot," Melora explained. "If you will tell your servant to pour in hot water and empty it again, Your Excellency—that is the first step in a good cup of tea." The *shaikh* gave the order.

"Next we measure the tea. A spoon for each cup, and one for the pot." She measured the size of the pot by eye and added the tea, while the *shaikh* watched her, bemused.

"And now it must steep for five minutes," Miss Trimmer said. "If you had a tea cosy, Your Excellency, it would keep the tea hot."

"What is this tea cosy?" he demanded.

"Why, a sort of little knitted hat for the pot."

"This sounds most bizarre!"

"Aye, and most practical, if you like a nice hot

cup," Trimmer assured him.

The *shaikh* turned to Leitrim. "You will procure for me the tea cosy, Leitrim, yes?"

"Certainly, Your Excellency."

"I shall knit you one, if Lord Leitrim will be kind enough to send my trunk along to the castle," Melora offered. She gave Leitrim a pert smile. "Now I have you at point non plus, milord. My gowns are not of sufficient importance to bestir you, but the *shaikh's* tea cosy will turn the trick."

Leitrim turned a frustrated face on her. "Baggage!" he growled under his breath.

"That is precisely what I am after—my baggage."

Trimmer sat regarding her watch, and when the proper time had passed she said to Melora, "Now you may pour."

Tea was poured and passed. The British contingent was careful not to destroy their brew with goat's milk. Trays of honeyed cakes, sugared dates and various sweets were passed by the servants and conversation was resumed.

"I heard at the *souk* the Reliant was attacked by pirates, Lord Leitrim," Monsieur Duval said. "That Rahma b. Jabir must be stopped. Lady Melora has been telling me of your gallant rescue operation."

Leitrim eyed him suspiciously. "Yes, I captured a dhow—bearing French armaments."

"They must be old ones. No French ships ply the waters since the war. War is a terrible thing. I wish the races could live in harmony. The Koran is at odds with the Bible on that point, I think, Your Excellency? 'Either go forth to war in separate parties, or go forth all together in a body.' "

"One must fight in a just cause," the *shaikh* replied.

A cynical smile curved Leitrim's lips. "When did you take up reading the Koran, Duval? Or the Bible, for that matter?"

"I learned the latter at my mother's knee. As to the Koran, why you can't spend long in Arabia without becoming intrigued with it. I am trying to get a crew together to translate it into idiomatic French, that my country might have the benefit of its wisdom. I have come to ask the *shaikh* if I might work with his *khalifah,* who is intimately knowledgeable in that field."

"Where does this scholarly work take place, at Raz-al-Khaimah?" Leitrim asked.

"I have rooms in the village," Duval replied blandly. He turned to the *shaikh*. "The work would progress more quickly if I had a cubbyhole here at the castle, with easy access to your *khalifah*—"

"Unfortunately, my *khalifah* is much preoccupied at the moment," the *shaikh* said. "He is a very holy man, close to *fana*. Such a man must turn away from the world, the better to find God. As to translating the Koran, I don't believe it is a solid idea. It is for Arabs. Every nation has its own prophets. You have your Jesus Christ, we our Mohammed. Each seeks the way in his own manner."

"If I could have just a word with him—" Duval insisted.

With a haughty, impatient, look, the *shaikh* changed the subject. From the divine, he turned his attention to more worldly matters. "I promised to show Lady Melora my pearls—the set Monsieur was speaking of a short while ago. I shall have them brought for your examination, ladies." He clapped his hands and sent for his major domo. The superior servant came and was sent for a jewel box.

When he returned, he handed the brass box to the *shaikh* with a bow. The box was ornate, like so many items in the castle. Roughly a foot long and a half as wide, it had a domed lid, the whole enamelled with intricate, writhing stems and flowers. He flipped the lid open and held out for display a king's ransom in jewels. The glitter of rubies and emeralds, of rings and necklaces and brooches was enough to dazzle an emperor.

"Oh my! How Prinney would love to get his hands on this lot!" Miss Trimmer exclaimed.

"We shall look with more detail another time," the *shaikh* said. "For the moment, it is the pearls I wish to show Lady—the ladies."

He extracted a red satin bag and shook out the necklace. A nest of large pearls glowed in the palm of his hand. He held it up, a lustrous strand of opera length.

"See the delicate tinge of rose—that play of color is called the pearl's orient," he explained. His words were directed at Melora, and as he spoke, he fondled the jewels with his long, fine fingers. "These are produced by the Mohar, a species of mollusk found only in the Persian Gulf. They are considered the finest pearls in the world. These were found in the fight between Oman and Qatar. It took ten years to assemble this perfectly matched set. They cost—but it is impolite, I believe, to discuss money in company."

Duval rose to examine them. "Look at the iridescence, the translucence. And the shape of each one is perfect. The pearl is an ancient symbol of perfection, Your Excellency."

"I know all about pearls," the *shaikh* replied comprehensively. "Pliny called them 'the richest merchandise of all.' "

"These will be worn by your wife, when you marry, sir?" Duval asked.

The *shaikh* gave him an enigmatic look and didn't reply directly. "Only by a lady of great importance, certainly. These are not a toy for a *houri*."

"What is a houri?" Melora asked.

The gentlemen exchanged a startled, conscious look.

Leitrim cleared his throat and said, "Miss Trimmer will explain later."

"Oh, one of *those*!" Melora said, and laughed. The *shaikh* cast a swift, reproving glare at her.

"Come now, Your Excellency," she said playfully, "You should not use words to make a lady blush. I maintain the solecism was yours. Am I not correct, gentlemen?" she asked the others.

"One never contradicts a lady," the *shaikh* bowed. His sudden fit of pique was gone as quickly as it came upon him. "To show my chagrin, you may try on the pearls, Lady Melora. This is not another solecism on my part, Lord Leitrim? Already I have disgraced myself once in this distinguished company. Allah forfend I should repeat my error."

"A fitting apology, Your Excellency," Leitrim nodded. And when did a *shaikh* ever apologize to anyone before!

Shaikh Rashid lifted the strand of pearls and went to attach them around Melora's throat. She helped him move aside the shawl from her shoulders. She was accutely conscious of the touch of his fingers on her skin—warm, brushing gently. His breaths fanned her cheek as he bent over her. A scent of musk and spice came from his robes. When the necklace was attached, he remained a moment, gazing at her. His eyes were like two black, glittering diamonds.

"You eclipse my other jewels, Lady Melora" he said softly.

A warm flush rose up the column of her throat. The breath caught in her lungs, and she could think of nothing to say, so she just smiled. The *shaikh* regarded her, unsmiling, then shook himself to attention. He moved aside to let the others see.

"*Enchantanté, n'est-çe-pas?*" he asked.

"*Formidable!*" Duval sighed. "The pearls are also very nice," he said, and laughed.

"Why thank you, monsieur!" Melora smiled. "That was a pretty compliment indeed. Trust the French!"

Duval wagged a playful finger at her. "Lord Leitrim will not agree with that sentiment, milady."

"But in the fine art of flirtation, monsieur, I'm sure even Lord Leitrim will admit the preeminence of the French."

"You put me to the test," Leitrim smiled lazily. "A hard compliment to outdo. How does one compare an Incomparable?"

Melora considered this and shook her head. "I expected better of an Englishman."

"But I am not English, Lady Melora. I am Irish."

"And not a drop of blarney in you! I listened for a silver tongue and found only a leaden echo," she scoffed playfully.

"Now that I can and must refute!" Leitrim exclaimed, his body assuming an alert attitude. "Leaden indeed! Where would England be without its Irish soldier, Wellington, to defend it? Its Irish statesman, Castlereagh to pilot the ship of state? The Irish Gunning ladies to add a little pulchritude, and the inimitable Tom Moore to write your songs?"

"Why we would have to rely on Lord Byron for our songs, would we not?" she answered lightly.

"And he, of course, is half Scotch on his mother's side!" Leitrim riposted.

"This amazes me!" the *shaikh* exclaimed, looking from one to the other with laughing eyes.

"What, that a lady is quick-witted enough to argue with a gentleman?" Melora asked.

"Argument requires no wit. It is instinctive to ladies. What amazes me is that you are permitted to argue with your men."

Leitrim gave Melora a triumphant grin. "Quite right sir. The young lady's wings must be clipped. She flies too high."

A soft smile glowed in the *shaikh's* lambent eyes as he gazed at Melora. "Let us spare her, Lord Leitrim. It would be a shame to trample that free spirit. It comes of our having permitted her to leave off her veil, don't you think?"

"I feel morally certain it would make no difference," Leitrim replied. "Her chatter would come through, loud and clear."

"I believe I shall take offense at this attack," Lady Melora decided, and rose grandly, smiling to show her pleasure at being the center of attention. "We shall go to our room and sulk, Miss Trimmer. Next time the gentlemen will not be so rough on us. Thank you for allowing me to try on your pearls, sir."

Leitrim breathed a sigh of relief that she was leaving, and rose punctiliously to his feet. Duval did likewise. The *shaikh* gave them a questioning look, and remained seated, as was his custom. He noticed the young lady's surprise that he should retain his seat when the other gentlemen rose. Perhaps in European company . . . He slowly rose to his feet and bowed.

Melora reached up and removed the pearls. She looked wistfully at their glowing beauty as she handed them back to the *shaikh*. He ran his fingers slowly over the smooth circles. "They are lovelier for having touched you," he said, and bowed again.

"Thank you, Your Excellency. That sounded amazingly French."

"That would be because I had a French tutor."

"And I a French nanny! We have more in common than we thought."

She curtsied, and left the room, followed by Trimmer. As they returned to their chamber, Melora was in high spirits. "Isn't he handsome, Trimmer?" she sighed.

"An excellent *parti*. And Ireland is not so very inconvenient. You would have a house in London for the Season."

"Ireland? I'm talking about the *shaikh*!"

"Then you are wasting your time, my girl. You

don't want to spend the rest of your life in this place, with no milk for your tea."

"I could live without milk. He speaks English very well."

Leitrim soon left the party to continue his letter. When Duval was alone with the *shaikh*, he turned a mischievous eye on his host. "A handsome gel," he said. "She takes your fancy, eh Shaikh?"

The *shaikh* gave him an offended look. "Lady Melora is a very important person. Do not speak of her in this light fashion. Her father is a man of immense influence in Britain."

"Why, her father has been dead for years. She was raised by an uncle of no particular importance. I daresay she'd never be missed if she didn't return."

The *shaikh* turned a sharp, questioning eye on Duval. "This is not what Leitrim has told me. The ladies are under his protection. I see what you are about, Duval. You wish to make trouble between the English and myself. This will not do, monsieur."

Duval hunched his shoulders. "I thought you had a taste for the young lady. Obviously you cannot marry her. She is a mighty attractive wench. Forward, of course."

"That is the English custom. It means nothing. She is a lady of unsullied reputation. It is unfortunate that she has the enticing behavior of a *houri* and excites a man's appetite, but—"

"Strange thing, reputations. A touch of scandal and phtt." Duval snapped his fingers. "She is finished. No decent man will have her. There is plenty of chance for scandal in such a place as this, *non*?"

The *shaikh* cast a commanding glare on his visitor. "I would take it very much amiss, however, if any scandal should attach to Lady Melora while she is under my protection. You understand me, monsieur?"

"Perfectly, Your Excellency."

"You may leave," the *shaikh* said, in an icy tone.

Duval left. His mind was alive with schemes to endear himself to Shaikh Rashid-al-Qasimi and thwart Lord Leitrim. If only he could stay at the castle. . . . When he had traveled beyond the gate, he was met by a ragged urchin who had been waiting for him. At first glance the urchin look Arabian, but a closer look revealed he was European.

"Did she say anything?" the young man asked.

"She didn't mention having seen you amongst the Arab prisoners aboard ship. I believe your secret is safe, Alphonse."

"She stared straight at me. I think we ought to get rid of her."

"Think again. She might prove more valuable alive than dead. The *shaikh* devours her with his eyes. His honor prevents his following the sane course, but he can't marry a foreigner, and after his passion comes to the boil . . . we shall see." Duval smiled a cunning smile and mounted his horse.

When Shaikh Rashid sat alone, he lifted the strand of pearls and rubbed them against his cheek. His eyes looked into the distance, seeing a vision of an enchanting lady with hair of gold and the bold, enticing smile of a *houri*. His body hungered for her, and the fact that she was unattainable only made her more irresistible. Regretfully, he returned the pearls to their pouch and called for his servant to take them away.

Chapter Six

Shaikh Rashid clapped his hands. The music ceased, dancing girls whirled out the door and he turned to his companion, Lord Leitrim. "Now it is time to discuss business," he said.

Coffee was brought in small cups. Leitrim rearranged himself on the cushion that served in lieu of a chair at the dinner table, and the *shaikh's* water pipe was brought. While the servants set it up, Leitrim lit a cigar.

As the smoke curled in circles over his head, he considered the best way to gain his end. "About the truce, Your Excellency," he began.

"It has been confirmed the pirate who attacked Lady Melora's ship was Rahma b. Jabir," the *shaikh* said. "He is not one of my people, but a Qawasim—what you call a Joasimee. I have no wish to go to war with the Joasimees. They would

66

object to my signing the truce—a blood bath would ensue, milord.''

"Rahma b. Jabir is an outlaw. The Joasimees wouldn't fight on his behalf. They're not doing much pirating nowadays.''

"They allow him to live at Raz-al-Khaimah.''

"You may be sure he pays handsomely for the privilege. We hoped you could convince the Joasimees to sign the truce as well. The other *shaikhs* look to you for guidance.'' Leitrim noticed the *shaikh's* pleasure in the compliment.

"This is true,'' Shaikh Rashid allowed. "I see that Britian has much to gain by the truce, but we are not a large trading nation, sir. Our people consider piracy not so much a crime as a sort of levy for using our waterway. In your England, the highways charge a toll to carriages, do they not?''

"For the upkeep of the roads, Your Excellency. The ocean requires no maintenance.''

"What of the upkeep of our people, milord? What do I gain for them by signing?''

"Peaceful navigation. India is a good market for you. There's a market in Britian as well for coffee, spices, pearls. Our European blockade is firmly in place in the Atlantic. If you wish to do any European trade, you will trade with England. The alternative you know—'' Leitrim disliked to make an outright threat. Rashid was clever enough to realize England was powerful. Retribution might be taken if the truce was not signed.

"Already you are at war with Napoleon. England has no ships or armies to spare.''

"We have alliances with other European powers. We don't fight Bonaparte alone. The piracy *will* stop, Your Excellency, with or without your help."

"The last alliance faltered—"

"That is why a new, stronger one is necessary. The petty *shaikhs* look to you for guidance," he repeated.

"Our people are nomads, Lord Leitrim. Shifting, like the sands of the desert. This truce you seek is illusory—a mirage."

"It is not the nomads that concern us, Shaikh Rashid, but the gentlemen who call themselves fishermen, who fish with guns and swords. You receive no booty from them. Why do you permit it?"

"Should I permit them to starve? The land is poor."

"A trading alliance with us is possible—and it would be profitable."

"I must discuss this with the other *shaikhs*. I shall write and arrange a meeting with Shaikh Murad. He also is influential and I must meet with him soon in any case. He wishes to make my sister his wife."

"Ayesha?" Lietrim asked. A quick frown flashed across his brow before he had time to get his emotions under control.

"I have only one sister, milord. An alliance between our two tribes would firm our friendship. And now I bid you goodnight."

The gentlemen rose and left the room together. They chatted on as they mounted the stairs. Lady Melora's room was to the right; Leitrim's to the left. Leitrim hesitated a moment, then turned left. He proceeded a few yards down the hall, then returned to the corner and peered around it.

Shaikh Rashid stood, watching from his dark, enigmatic eyes.

Leitrim came forward sheepishly. "Just going to say goodnight to the ladies," he said. "It is the custom."

"Excellent. I too shall honor this foreign custom," the *shaikh* replied, and fell into step with Leitrim. "It has come to my attention that Lady Melora is an orphan," he said, and gave his companion a questioning look. "The highly placed gentleman, her father, whom you spoke of—"

Duval, making mischief! "Miss Trimmer informed me this is true. I hadn't been aware of it. Her father is dead, but when a lady is related by blood to half the aristocracy of Europe, we do not call her an orphan. Marriage between the noble families is a long-standing tradition. Lady Melora is related to the British House of Hanover, and through the marriage of a cousin, to the Austrian House of Hapsburg as well," he invented, to put the seal on her importance.

Leitrim tapped at the door and Miss Trimmer went to admit him. Over her shoulder, Melora looked up from a book and smiled.

"We shan't disturb you. We've just come to say goodnight, ladies," Leitrim said.

Melora came forward. "Pray come in," she smiled.

"No, no. It would be too farouche to disturb you at this hour."

"It's only nine o'clock!" Melora exclaimed. "We are bored to flinders. Do come in." She cast a winning smile at the *shaikh*, who looked a question at Leitrim.

"Another time," Leitrim said firmly. He bowed and turned away.

The *shaikh* bowed and, with a regretful sigh, left with Leitrim. "It is the custom to refuse such an invitation?" he asked wistfully.

"Yes. Custom decrees that the lady must invite one in, but after dinner, one must refuse," he said, with a face as stiff as a poker.

They parted at the corner to go to their respective rooms.

"Well, that's odd!" Melora said to a frowning Trimmer. "Why did they come, if they didn't mean to visit us?"

"Probably some Arab custom," Miss Trimmer replied. "I wish we had something to read. These books are very petty, but I would give my left arm for a good gothic novel by Miss Radcliffe. I have three in my trunks."

"We can't retire at nine o'clock. I'm going to continue my letter to Arabella."

Lady Melora settled herself at the desk and took up her quill. 'What a mad, mad time we are having,' she wrote. 'Shaikh Rashid held an international party for us today. A most charming French gentleman was there, Monsieur Duval by name. The *shaikh* and Lord Leitrim just left our apartment. After they stayed an age, we finally had to push them out the door by main force, or they would have stayed half the night.'

She read what she had written and frowned. "It is impossible to make bricks without straws," she said, and threw the quill aside. "Well, I daresay nine-fifteen is not too early to retire."

After her early night, she was awake bright and early in the morning. She was standing at the window, looking once more at the ocean and the sky, when there was a tap at the door. Trimmer opened it, and Lord Leitrim stepped in. He was alone this time.

Melora turned from the window and said, "Good morning," in a noticeable tone of pique.

"It's a fine day," Leitrim said.

"Yes, such a fine day it seems a shame to spend it locked up in a castle."

"You make yourself sound like the doomed princess in a fairytale. What you require, my girl, is a Prince Charming."

"Preferably one who will release me from my prison."

"Mediocre minds must think alike. That is the very reason I am here. Will a dhow do in place of a milk-white steed?"

A brilliant smile greeted the suggestion. "Even a dog cart would suit me. Where are we going?"

"Somewhere that we can be alone, and talk."

Her brows lifted in surprise. "Alone?"

"Away from the *shaikh*, is all I mean. Naturally Miss Trimmer will accompany us."

Miss Trimmer was less than thrilled to be dragooned on to a dhow, but she didn't care to remain behind alone, so she agreed to accompany them. As soon as they stepped out into the sunlight, she began complaining. "You must stay away from that nasty Hormuz place where the pirates attack, Leitrim. You won't be around to rescue us this time—from another ship, I mean."

"We aren't setting out to sea, Trimmer," he assured her. "They'll know I have no valuable cargo aboard in any case."

Melora gave him a cool look. "Only our valueless selves, Miss Trimmer," she snipped. "Lord Leitrim doesn't consider us worth pirating."

After a few more complaints about the heat, the wet sand that was destroying her slippers and the wind that would no doubt seek her out as soon as they left dry land, Miss Trimmer allowed herself to be aided into the dhow. It was a long, light wooden craft rigged with sails. A few British seamen were aboard to sail the ship.

"Can we go below to get out of the sun and wind?" Miss Trimmer asked, as soon as they were afloat.

"Trimmer!" Melora exclaimed. "You can't be serious. We've been locked up for a week. When we finally get out for a day, you want to sit in a cabin." She looked around at the sea, the receding coastline. She felt the fresh breeze on her brow, and determined to stay on deck.

"We'll just go below for a moment and settle Miss Trimmer in," Leitrim decided. "I wish I could offer you tea, ma'am. Or even wine. Unfortunately all we have aboard is rum."

"Rum? What does it taste like?"

"It's made from sugar cane—a rough drink. I wouldn't recommend it for a lady."

"A little sugar water will do me no harm. I'll try a glass," Trimmer decided.

Leitrim reluctantly sent off for a bottle and glasses. Melora, always eager for a new experience, wanted to taste it too. The brown liquor was tasted neat first.

"This is dreadful stuff," Miss Trimmer decided. "It would eat your stomach out if taken straight. Have you no water aboard?"

Water was sent for, and while they had their

drink, Leitrim decided to get the lecture over with, so that they might enjoy the rest of the trip.

"I want to talk about yesterday's tea party," he said.

"Delightful, was it not?" Miss Trimmer smiled, and drank her rum.

"Not for me," Leitrim scowled. "I warned you about throwing your bonnet at the *shaikh*, Lady Melora. I don't want you stirring up any mischief with him at this time. That is French for saying you mustn't set up a flirtation with him."

"The French would never say such a thing!" Miss Trimmer assured him. "They are all for romance."

A spark of anger flashed in Melora's eyes. "And if he should decide to initiate one with me, should I not conciliate him—for the sake of the truce, milord?" she asked.

"I don't advise you to make a pawn of yourself in this game, madam. You know what happens to pawns. They're dispensable. It is their fate to be the first pieces taken in the game."

"I never could understand chess," Miss Trimmer said, and added a little rum to her glass.

Melora cast him a scathing glance. "It is the pawns' relative immobility that accounts for it. Don't think to immure us in the castle forever while you enjoy yourself. I heard the music coming from the dining room last night, and saw the dancing girls enter."

"You shouldn't have been out of your room! What has *my* behavior to do with anything? I hope you aren't putting yourself on an equal footing with a bunch of dancing girls! You might be interested to hear your reputation has already taken a downturn—thanks to Monsieur Duval. He told Shaikh Rashid your father is dead.''

"Why would he do such a thing?" Miss Trimmer demanded. Melora too looked with interest for his answer.

"Why do you think? To lessen your importance, and the degree of respect that must be shown to you. I've convinced Shaikh Rashid you are unexceptionable. If he inquires for your cousins, the King and Queen of Britian, don't be in too great a hurry to disillusion him. I also told him you're kin to the Hapsburgs. We're all related, if we go back to Adam and Eve.''

"A half-Hanoverian and a perHapsburg— why did you not make me a Bourbon while you're about it? I at least had a French governess, and can speak the language.''

"Duval would know it isn't true," Leitrim replied. "I'm sorry to see he's permitted to run tame at the castle. He's up to no good. You noticed he was trying to get himself battened on Shaikh Rashid.''

"What have you against Duval?" Miss Trimmer asked.

"His nationality—and a few other things. He arrived here a year ago in possession of a handsome dhow. The ship disappeared in one of the thousands of inlets around Raz-al-Khaimah. I wager it's outfitted with guns and a pirate crew by now. The man isn't even a French patriot. He's a freebooter. He originally came looking for pearls, but soon realized where a greater fortune could be made. He wouldn't balk at using a lady, if he saw any way to turn a penny on you," he warned Melora. "Forewarned is forearmed.''

"And he looking as though he wouldn't melt in butter. I thought he was studying theology!" Miss Trimmer said, and took another quaff of her rum.

Leitrim snorted.

"You need not concern yourself about our falling into any intimacy with Duval," Melora pointed out. "Where would we see him?"

"He's the sort who is always slithering around, trying to ingratiate himself."

"I know the kind," Miss Trimmer said. Her voice was becoming heavy. "Give him a mile and he'll take an inch. And speaking of inches, Leitrim, when are we to get our trunks? I have worn this wretched old bombazine till it thinks it is a second skin, and Melora is most eager to show off her pretty gowns to the *shaikh*."

Regarding Leitrim's furrowed brow, Melora said, "*That's* why you're keeping our trunks from us! You *want* me to look plain in front of him!"

"I don't want you flaunting yourself in the immodest clothing ladies wear in England," he admitted.

Trimmer shook her head and smiled into her glass. "Closing the barn horse after the door. . . . He is already in love with her, Leitrim. Did you not see how he looked when he put the pearls around her throat? 'They are lovelier for having touched you,' he said."

"I'm not deaf!" Leitrim snapped.

"Good, then you also heard me promise the *shaikh* a tea cosy," Melora reminded him. "He might take offense if I fail to produce it. Could we not go to the shipyard now and get our trunks?"

"No."

"What will Melora wear when the *shaikh* lends

her a mount? He has promised to, you recall,"
Trimmer reminded him.

"Perhaps Leitrim can lend me a pair of
trousers," Melora suggested.

Leitrim's eyes rolled ceilingward in dismay.
"Why not just go in your petticoats, if it's your
intention to make a cake of yourself?"

"My petticoats, alas! are not fit to be seen—all
splattered in mud. So unless you wish me to play
Lady Godiva, I hope you can get my trunks."

"I'll get you a *burnous*—and a veil. They'll
provide some protection against the sun and wind.
You don't want to destroy your fair English
complexion. It is half what attracts the *shaikh's*
interest."

Melora smiled into the distance. "Do you know,
Leitrim, I think it is the *shaikh's* dusky coloring
and flashing black eyes that make him so irresistible to me too."

A peculiar smile twisted Leitrim's lips. "I know
what you mean."

"I knew it!" Melora exclaimed. "You *are*
interested in Ayesha! I've seen you mooning after
her. I'm not surprised. Opposites do attract, folks
say."

Leitrim scowled. "And birds of a feather roost
together. A dove has no place in the hawk's nest."

She gave him a teasing smile. "Don't be silly.
Rashid is safe with me. I wouldn't hurt him for the
world."

"I wish I could be quite certain the reverse is
true."

"But I told you—I thrive on danger. Unlike
some people," she added with a taunting smile.

"I, of course, joined the Bombay Buccaneers for

the peace and quiet. I have warned you—"

"Twice now! Your caveat is recorded, milord. I shall deal most discreetly and politely with the desert hawk. With a mere Irish popinjay, however, there is no need for such caution. This rum is horrid, and I want to go up on deck. Are you all right here alone, Miss Trimmer?"

"I'm fine, dear. You run along," Miss Trimmer said, and reached for the rum bottle. Leitrim removed it from the table and took Melora away.

"Where are we going?" she asked, when they reached the deck.

"I thought you might like to see the coral reefs. They grow along this stretch of coast." He peered over the railing. "There—we're passing them now."

Melora looked where he was pointing, and saw what looked like pale green clouds under the darker green of the water. "Isn't that strange!" she exclaimed. "And how pretty. Is that the same sort of coral we give babies for teething?"

"That's it, only they polish away the rough edges for babies, of course. It's used for building in this part of the world too. There's a deal of it used in Shaikh Rashid's castle."

"What is it made of?"

"It's the petrified skeletons of marine polyps."

Melora wrinkled her nose. "You mean it's a fish cemetery! Ugh! And we give that to babies to put in their mouths? Oh look, Leitrim! That growth looks like a whale! See the sloping body, and the tail fanning out just so."

Leitrim peered skeptically into the depths. "I doubt it's a whale skeleton."

As the ship passed beyond the coral reefs,

Melora looked up at the cloudless sky, felt the cooling breeze on her cheeks, and drew a luxurious sigh. "Isn't it lovely here. Why don't you ask Ayesha to marry you, Leitrim? I shall marry Shaikh Rashid, and we'll all live happily ever after."

He gave her a sad smile. "Don't think it hasn't occurred to me! I'm not immune to the attraction of opposites. But it wouldn't do. Ayesha would never fit into my life in Ireland, and I couldn't remain here."

"You could renounce your title and estate."

"Yes, and live on my brother-in-law's charity. Charming."

"I didn't think of that."

"There are a lot of things you haven't thought of, I fear. You wouldn't fit in here either. You'd be a fish out of water. Why don't you just enjoy the sojourn for what it is—a brief Arabian adventure."

"Perhaps you're right," she said consideringly. "But what's an adventure without some romance, Leitrim? You have your company business to employ your mind. My major business in life is to find the right man, and inveigle the poor unfortunate into marrying me. I am just going about my business."

"One could wish you had a wiser mentor than Miss Trimmer."

"She suits me very well. I can always wind her round my finger."

"Just as I feared," he said wearily. "It will be for me to play the role of tyrant."

"You play it exceedingly well, sir, but don't

mistake me for one of your seamen."

"Not even when you eventually talk me into permitting you to wear trousers shall I make that mistake."

She gave him a pert smile. "Such persuading wouldn't be necessary if you'd get our trunks."

"I look forward to your persuasions, Lady Melora."

He put his hand on her elbow and they walked to the bow to catch the breeze, till Miss Trimmer staggered up from below. She held a bottle of rum, and her steps were unsteady.

"Where the devil did she get that?" Leitrim exclaimed, running after her.

Melora ran after him. "It seems Miss Trimmer has been doing some persuading of her own. One of the sailors must have given it to her."

Miss Trimmer turned a glazed eye on Leitrim and demanded, "What are you up to, eh? Abandoning me in that foul hole while you cuddle my charge! And why have you got two heads, Leitrim? Oh, you are twins. I'm sorry, gentlemen," she said, shaking her head in confusion.

Leitrim gave Melora a questioning look. "Does this happen often?" he demanded.

"No, she usually drinks tea."

"We'll blame it on the rum. We had best get her below before she falls overboard."

Melora took one arm, Leitrim the other and between them they got her in the cabin. "We'd best get her home," Leitrim decided.

"I'll stay with her," Melora said.

"Pity. The conversation was just becoming

interesting.''

With a light laugh, Leitrim left, and Melora began scolding her derelict chaperone.

Chapter Seven

An early night was necessary after Miss Trimmer's excesses. The only excitement of the next day was the arrival of the ladies' trunks.

"I asked Captain Redding to send them over when I went to arrange for the dhow yesterday," Leitrim explained.

"I shall begin the *shaikh's* tea cosy," Miss Trimmer said. Leitrim gave her a questioning look. "That is, I'll just cast on the stitches for you, Melora."

"I know how to knit!" Melora assured him.

"Yes my dear, but we don't want to give the nice *shaikh* a tawdry thing, full of dropped stitches," Trimmer said. "I shall do it, and let you hold the knitting if he drops in this evening."

"Then I shall unpack our trunks."

Almost immediately, Ayesha's female servants came giggling and whispering into the room to perform this service for them. Leitrim looked hopefully for a sign of Ayesha. Finding none, he soon left.

The girls looked in surprise at the gowns, held them up at the mirror, wondering at the fitted waists and lack of arms. They stared at Melora's hair and eyes, her pale skin, wondering amongst themselves what their master saw in such a pale woman, with skin like milk, and a body that would not provide him with hearty sons. Allah be praised. It was well he must marry a *real* woman soon, to rid his mind of this pallid sorceress.

There was no company that evening, but Melora received a note from Shaikh Rashid, telling her he was taking her for a ride in the desert the next morning. "And he's arranged a light carriage for you, Miss Trimmer," she said, smiling at the note.

"Oh dear. That sound exceedingly hot and uncomfortable—the desert," Trimmer complained. "Could he not take us shopping instead? I hunger for the sight of a store. It is so vexing not being able to spend any money."

"I doubt our English currency would be acceptable here. We can go shopping any time. When shall we ever have another chance to ride in the desert?"

Miss Trimmer looked up from her knitting and said with great feeling, "Never, I hope."

"We must take every opportunity to experience life here. I still have to see a mosque, and ride a camel. I wonder what I should wear tomorrow."

Melora was wearing her English riding habit the next morning when Leitrim dropped in to see them off, but she wasn't sure she did the right thing.

Leitrim frowned in dissatisfaction with the whole affair. "He didn't even ask me if I would like to come along," he said. "No doubt it's just a brief outing. He can't be planning to take you far if Miss Trimmer is accompanying you in a carriage."

"The shorter, the better," Trimmer said.

"Ayesha is accompanying us," Melora taunted. "Perhaps that is why he didn't ask you along. We were just trying to decide what I should wear," she said, looking for his opinion.

"Of course you must wear the *burnous.*" But the riding habit suited her perfectly. Blue was her color, and the habit was a particularly lovely shade of cornflower blue. "That woolen habit will not only suffocate you with heat in the desert, it will annoy the *shaikh.*"

Melora gave him a knowing smile. "I think not. Rashid likes me for being different." She picked up the dashing bonnet that completed the outfit and looked at it uncertainly.

"Yes, but you will be out in public today. What passes for acceptable within the walls of his own castle won't necessarily do abroad."

"Thus far," she said coldly, "you have misdirected me on every detail regarding my behavior to Rashid. 'Don't speak,' you told me. 'Cover your face. Don't stick your nose beyond the door of this room.' Yet the *shaikh* was swift to allow me those freedoms you denied. I begin to wonder just which of you two gentlemen is the monster."

She perched the bonnet on her head and looked in the mirror to adjust it. "The headdress, Trimmer," she called over her shoulder. Trimmer handed her the white shawl. "I shall wear this

concession to Arabia, because of the sun's heat.
Not becuase the *shaikh*—or you—say so.''

Leitrim spoke to Trimmer in a low voice. ''I
should have insisted she not wear the riding habit.
Next time I'll know how to handle her.''

He accompanied Miss Trimmer and Lady
Melora to the *shaikh's* quarters, where Melora had
the exquisite pleasure of hearing Rashid say, ''Excellent! I hoped you would come *à l'anglaise*. What
a pity you must mar your charming outfit with the
head shawl, but it will serve better than a bonnet in
the sun and sand.''

''What time will you be back?'' Leitrim asked. A
trace of anxiety was noticeable.

''Travel in the heat of day will be uncomfortable
for the ladies,'' the *shaikh* told him. ''By leaving
early this morning we miss the worst of it. We shall
ride home in the cool of the evening.''

''You can't keep them in the desert all day.''

''That is not my intention. Do not concern yourself, Lord Leitrim. We are riding with a guard of
half a dozen men, and Miss Trimmer is along for
propriety.''

He put a hand on Melora's elbow and led her
and Miss Trimmer out of the castle, around to his
stable, where Ayesha joined them. The pungent
smell of horses caused Melora a wave of nostalgia
as she looked in admiration at the well set-up
building. The *shaikh's* stables were as well-built as
most homes, and had as many grooms as a large
house has servants. They moved quietly about their
chores, grooming, brushing, watering the beautiful
animals, with gracefully curved necks and gleaming
flanks. There were a dozen blood horses in all,

their hides groomed to a glow. Their manes and tails were worn long, floating in the breeze as they pranced in their eagerness for excitement. She noticed they were tied by the rear leg, rather than around the neck. Rashid had all colors, bays and grays and chestnut, and one jet black stallion called Midnight.

"The taproots of your English thoroughbreds come from Arabia," he said proudly. "Desert-bred horses are the best. Though light, they have the speed, the stamina and endurance required for racing. This beauty is my prize broodmare," he said, stroking the neck of a handsome bay. "I call her Scheherezade, because she has spawned a thousand and one stories for her prowess. I was offered twenty-five thousand pounds for her."

"Good gracious! That's a fortune!" Melora gasped.

"True, but one offspring sells for ten thousand. She will give birth to more than two and a half foals, *n'est-ce-pas*?"

Melora looked over the mounts to choose hers. She spotted a sleek bay mare. "Oh, what a lovely mare! May I have her, Your Excellency?"

He bowed his permission. "She is Désirée, Scheherezade's daughter," he said. "See how intelligent and expressive her eyes are. She likes you already. A fine mount—long muscles, good spirit." He tossed his head, and a servant came forward to help Melora mount the mare.

Ayesha and Miss Trimmer were assisted up into a carriage somewhat resembling an English curricle, except that it had a roof for protection against the sun, and a separate seat for the driver.

The *shaikh* mounted a frolicsome gray gelding, who pranced in his eagerness to be off. As promised, half a dozen of the *shaikh's* men mounted and followed them as they rode beyond the gates into the desert. Shaikh Rashid rode at the front of his men, side-by-side with Melora.

Leitrim watched them leave from a window at the top of the castle. Though he was a keen admirer of horses, he took no pleasure from the sight of the caravan setting off on this particular voyage.

"I feel like a Captain of Dragoons," Melora smiled. "Shall we gallop, Rashid? I know that is the Arabian's best pace."

"If you wish, it will be best to gallop now, while the air is cool. Later we must go more slowly, to save our horses."

The initial gallop over the sparkling sand was invigorating. Here at the edge of the desert, there was still some vegetation. Wild grass grew, and an occasional shrub dotted the path. As they progressed, the vegetation petered out, and before them stretched an ocean of sand, rippled to waves by the wind.

Suddenly aware of their isolation, Melora said, "We're leaving your sister and Miss Trimmer far behind."

"They will take a slightly different—shorter—route. Don't be concerned for them." But the gallop was cut to a canter. As they progressed, the sun rose higher; the heat became greater, and the horses continued on a steady pace. There was no sign of the carriage now. Melora's concern began mounting to worry. She wished she had worn the *burnous,* that would allow a breeze. Her throat became parched, and even with a veil covering her nose and mouth, she could taste the sand.

Surely he would stop soon—for a rest, a drink of water. She knew the men carried water with them. Glancing to her companion, she saw only the stark profile of Shaikh Rashid, indifferent as the desert. His head was held high, even in this awful heat. A frisson of fear scuttled up her spine.

The heat intensified till it was like an oven. Melora's tight-fitting, blue habit soaked up the sun. Perspiration wet her brow and trickled down her forehead. Across her shoulders the sun burned like a brand. Her arms were tired, her fingers were frozen in one position, her whole body ached with fatigue. When she looked at Rashid, he seemed oblivious to the discomfort. No moisture beaded his brow as he gazed into the infinite distance—sand as far as the eye could see. And no one to help her, if he should decide to—no, she wouldn't think that.

Overhead, the sun continued to beat down. It rose up from the white sands in a wavy curtain, blinding in its brightness. There was nothing but sky and sun and sand. She felt she had ridden into the entranceway of hell. How did the horses stand it? How much longer could she go on? She cast a frightened glance at Rashid.

"You are not tired—not too hot?" he asked. She caught a glint of something in his eyes—a calculating look that spelled danger. He had purposely drawn her away from the other ladies. She was at his mercy, surrounded by his men.

It wouldn't be wise to show her fear. "Not at all, Your Excellency," she said firmly.

His lips curved in a laughing smile that set her quaking inside. "Well done, Lady Melora."

Then he urged his mount on to a gallop. Escape was impossible, so she dug her heel into Désirée's side and kept pace with him, across the endles sands, with the men following behind. The sun climbed in the sky, a gigantic ball of fire floating in the azure void. She was proud of her endurance, determined to show no fear or pain, yet the physical discomfort was becoming intolerable. Surely he must stop soon.

Melora was about to beg him to rest, when it happened. A picture appeared on the horizon, clear yet insubstantial, of date trees and a lake of water. She could almost feel the water's welcome coolness.

"What's that?" she demanded.

"You see something? It must be a mirage. It happens often in the desert. It is said one sees what one is dreaming of. What do you see, Melora?"

She stared into the distance. There by the lake, amidst the date trees, she saw herself and Rashid—clearly. They were alone in the oasis, going toward the water.

"Water," she said.

"Perhaps you are thirsty? Another mile along there is an oasis. We shall stop there."

She looked again at her mirage. It was gone. That image that had seemed so sharp she could touch it had vanished like smoke. Soon the real oasis appeared, a black patch on the horizon at first, that gradually assumed the shape of trees. The horses, smelling water, increased their pace. Within minutes, they had reached a spot of magic green in the white ocean of desert. Rashid lifted her down from Désirée. She was finished with pride. She welcomed his assistance, for she knew if she tried to get down by herself, her legs would fold under her.

"I'm a little stiff," she admitted.

Rashid's black diamond eyes smiled into hers. He set her feet on the ground, but his hands stayed at her waist. "You are *formidable*, Lady Melora. Grown men have begged for mercy on that ride, but you! You are the Queen of the Desert!" And still he kept his hands on her, held her with his glittering eyes.

Her breaths came in quick gasps. Oh God, what would he do next? "Were you testing me?" she asked, and removed his hands.

He didn't put up any fight. "Come, we drink. I am parched." He seized a goatskin bag from a servant.

"Like so," he said, and held the bag aloft to show her how to drink. The cool water ran in a spout, glinting like liquid silver, to be caught in his open mouth. Laughing, he let the water spill over his face. In the shade of the date trees, he pulled off his head covering and poured water over his head, laughing. There seemed a frenzy in that laugh.

Melora was given another of the water bags, and drank thirstily. She caught the water in her hands and patted it on her fevered brow.

"We rest now for thirty minutes," Rashid announced, and led her toward a lean-to, placed amidst the trees, while the men watered the horses. Why was he separating her from the others? And what difference did it make? They were his men.

"Will that give the others time to catch up with

us?'' she asked, feigning indifference.

"We shall join them later. This heat is too much for ordinary ladies.''

"So you are testing me, eh?'' she demanded. "Why did you do that?''

Rashid peeled a fig and handed it to her. "I wished to learn whether Lady Melora was—how do you say it in England? Up to scratch.'' His eyes burned into hers.

"That was a sly trick, sir,'' she said, trying for a playful air. "And we still have to repeat the ride home.''

"But no! Whatever of the formidable Lady Melora, *I* could not perform that tremendous feat twice in one day.''

Her eyes widened in alarm and her heart pounded mercilessly. "Surely you don't mean we must remain overnight!''

"No, no. Lord Leitrim—he would call out the British Army. We shall return by the shorter route, along the coast.''

She suspected a trick. "Shorter route—along the coast?''

"You wished to see our desert, did you not? You have seen it. You have *conquered* it!'' he declared.

Melora examined the fig and bit daintily into it. It gave her an excuse to be silent, and a chance to think. Was this a test, or an excuse? And why would he test her unless . . . Was it possible he was thinking of making her his wife?

"We are very close to where I train my falcons,'' Rashid said. "You would like to see them?''

The mounting fear subsided. "I would love to.''

"First we must pass through a little village, with a mosque, then two miles further—''

"Oh, may I go in the mosque?" she asked eagerly.

Rashid looked stunned. "But no! Women are not permitted. Only men are allowed."

"You don't allow women to practice their religion?" she asked, shocked.

"They do so in private."

"What about marriage and christenings—aren't they even allowed in the mosque for their wedding?"

"The mosque is not precisely like your Christian church. The world *masjid*—mosque—means 'a place of prostration' to God. It is only a place for praying."

"Couldn't I just have a quick peep in the door? I should love to see inside a mosque."

"There is very little to see. There are no statues or pictures, as in your church. No hymns—well, parts of the Koran are chanted, but there is no music. Not even chairs or pews. Just an open space, covered with mats and carpets, with a *mihrab*—a sort of niche—for the holy man who leads the prayer. There is a set of steps with a seat on top that is used by the preacher."

"If no one knew I was a woman—" she said hopefully.

Rashid shook his head firmly. "I would know. And Allah would know. Do not try my patience too far," he said haughtily.

Caught between fear and anger, she acquiesced, but the more he forbade it, the more determined she was to get inside a mosque. The rest was soon over, and they continued on their way. When Melora saw that sulking did her no good, she gave it up. The remainder of the trip was short. They left the desert and went directly to the *shaikh's* hunting lodge. She could smell water in the distance, and knew by the trees that the coast was not far away. Rashid had taken her in a circle through the desert.

"You go and freshen up," he said. "I shall speak to my trainers and return for you."

Miss Trimmer and Ayesha were taking their ease in a comfortable little parlor, sipping lemonade and eating fruit. "What has taken you such an age?" Miss Trimmer demanded. "I am bored to death. Ayesha, you know, speaks no English, though she smiles and pretends to understand what I am saying."

"I've conquered the desert, Miss Trimmer," Melora said proudly. "And now Shaikh Rashid is going to show me his falcons. Isn't it exciting?"

"You look worn to the socket."

"I'm a little tired," she admitted, and drank deeply of the cool drink. Rashid joined them for lunch. He said a few words to his sister, who made a low murmur in reply. Melora tried to see the woman through her veil. She disliked to stare, but thought Leitrim was right in thinking her attractive. The eyes especially, so dark and glowing, were beautiful.

After they had rested, the *shaikh* took them all out to where his falcons roosted on perches atop tall poles. The falconers came forward, carrying hooded birds on their wrists, which were protected by padded gloves. The hoods were ornamented with embroidery, that provided a sort of crown to the birds' dull plumage. The man in charge wore a silver whistle around his neck. He handed Shaikh Rashid a padded glove and he slid it on his left hand.

From each bird's leg a bell was suspended. The bells tinkled as the birds moved.

"What are the bells for?" Miss Trimmer asked.

"For ballast in flight," the *shaikh* explained. "They're belled as soon as we capture them. Each bell has a different tone, to help us distinguish them. These leg straps—they're called jesses—are attached to hold the tethering rope. As he spoke, he took the falcon on to his padded wrist, twining the jesses between his fingers. "Here, my sweet. Come to your perch," he crooned gently.

"Are these peregrine falcons?" Melora asked. "They're lighter in color than ours at home."

"Yes, desert peregrines. We like long-winged birds here in the open country. We only use the female—she's larger and bolder than the tercel. This one is in splendid feather."

Shaikh Rashid turned to speak to his servants. The servants moved away toward a growth of trees and bushes, beating a tambourine-like instrument as they went. A large gray-brown bird rose into the sky, with a slow but powerful beating of its wings.

Rashid lifted the falcon high on his wrist, removed the hood and cast loose the jesses. He shouted encouragingly at the bird and it soared up after its prey. An echo of the tinkling bell hung on the air. The other falcons caught the scent and became restive.

The freed falcon made a few circles, then her keen eye caught the quarry and her powerful wings increased the pace of their beating. With quick strokes she began to hone in on the bustard. The bustard strained forward. She had got underway, and her powerful wings carried her higher. Higher the birds flew, smaller falcon swooping after the larger bird.

"It's horrid," Miss Trimmer muttered. "I hope the bustard gets away."

Rashid turned and gave an incredulous little laugh. It sounded almost cruel. Melora looked at him, then turned away to examine the birds closer at hand. When Rashid emitted a triumphant shout, she glanced up. The falcon swooped in for the kill. Her sharp talons clawed into the quarry's back, her beak seemed to poke into the bird. The bustard made a convulsive movement with her wings, then plummeted to earth. The falcon soared off into the blue, circled a moment, then swooped back to Rashid's wrist to be rewarded.

"Doesn't she retrieve her prey?" Melora asked.

"A falcon? No, she's not a tame bird. You can never train them to retrieve. That's for dogs." But it was his servant who ran after the bustard and brought back the victim.

"Would you like to try it?" Rashid asked Melora. "I have a haggard at roost who's not very ferocious."

Melora was very tired from the ride, and chose to watch Rashid. More bustards were beat out of the bushes. Rashid and his trainer both freed falcons, to show her how well-trained they were, each choosing his own prey and going after it unswervingly.

When the demonstration was over, Melora suggested they should return home. "It's getting rather late," she pointed out. The brilliant sun was lowering in the sky.

"You're tired," he said, chagrined at his thoughtlessness.

"I'm afraid Miss Trimmer is."

"She and Ayesha have had an easy day. You shall ride in the carriage on the return trip. Ayesha will be happy for the chance to ride."

Melora was pleased on two scores. It gave her a chance to rest, and provided some companionship for Trimmer.

"I shall be glad to get home," Miss Trimmer said, as soon as the carriage was off. A few of the horses galloped on ahead, but Rashid and his sister walked at a leisurely pace with the carriage.

"Oh but hasn't it been exciting, Miss Trimmer? I wonder how far we are from the castle."

"Quite a few miles, and it's already twilight. We shan't be home before dark."

"I'm rather hungry. Rashid hardly ate anything when we stopped at his hunting box, or whatever he calls it. He must be ravenous."

"What is that up ahead? It looks like a fire!" Miss Trimmer demanded, clutching at Melora's elbow. It was now dark enough that the flames stood out against the night.

Rashid pulled alongside the carriage and said, "We shall stop soon, ladies. The servants are preparing a fire and making supper for us."

"How lovely!" Melora said.

"We are so close to home, we might as well go on and eat in peace. But it is nice and cool here," Trimmer decided.

When she saw the blankets and pillows ranged around the fire, she decided she approved of the plan. "He has arranged all this well in advance," she pointed out to her charge. "So thoughtful. And look, he has made tea for me! Now that is the very sort of little gesture that shows true consideration. I can almost forgive him for killing the birds.''

"Why Trimmer, at home all the gentlemen hunt! I never heard you complain about our friends and relatives killing rabbits.''

"Please, dear, don't speak of such things when we are about to eat.''

It was unfortunate that fowl was on the menu, but there were also seafood and rice and a tempting variety of fruit. Ayesha took charge of the picnic in her quiet way, and Rashid saw to the ladies' comfort. It was strange and romantic, eating by firelight across from the *shaikh*. He was very attentive to all Melora's desires, peeling fruit for her, and not forgetting Miss Trimmer either.

When the meal was done and the servants were putting everything away, Rashid said to Melora, "Would you like to take a little walk before we leave—stretch your legs?''

The moonlight was bright, adding its pale illumination to the firelight. They walked a little apart from the group, and stopped by a rock. Melora leaned against it and sighed luxuriously at the moon.

"It's been a wonderful day. Thank you. I shall never forget it.''

"Nor I, Melora.''

"I can smell something sweet in the air. Is it flowers?'' she asked, looking all around.

On the left, a small bush with a gnarled and twisted root had put forth a few flowers. "It's coming from there. What is it?''

Rashid picked the flower and brought it to her. "I am not well informed on flowers. That is ladies' work, but it smells like a clove. The spice grows on such a plant. This one is a poor wild, stunted thing."

Melora put it to her face and inhaled deeply. "How romantic! The spices of Araby! I shall press this and keep it for a souvenir."

Rashid gazed at her. "Souvenir—that is French for memory. Don't remember me by a dead, dry flower. I shall give you a better sourvenir, Lady Melora."

She looked at him questioningly. "What?"

"We must think of something suitable," he said. "And now I believe your Miss Trimmer is eager to get home." He took her arm and escorted her back to the carriage. For the remainder of the trip, he rode silently beside them. Melora took the fanciful notion he was thinking what souvenir would be suitable. Or perhaps whether a souvenir would be necessary at all. A souvenir was only necessary if she should be leaving.

Leitrim, pacing his room, went to visit the ladies as soon as they reached their chamber.

"Tell me all about your day," he demanded.

"It was thrilling!" Melora said. But she was tired now, and all she wanted was to get out of her hot riding habit and into a cool tub of water.

Leitrim narrowed his eyes and studied her. She looked fatigued. "Did Rashid, by any chance, take you the long way around?" he asked.

"We took a little detour through the desert," she replied nonchalantly. "It was fascinating. I saw a mirage, and we stopped at an oasis."

"Good God!" Leitrim exclaimed. "He took you that far—the oasis is miles into the desert. We can stop worrying that he's trying to court you! Kill you is more like it.''

She glared at his laughing face. "On the contrary. I believe he was testing me to see if I could stand up to the rigors of desert life on a permanent basis, Leitrim. He found me formidable. In fact, he called me the Queen of the Desert. What would a *shaikh's* wife be called, Miss Trimmer?'' she asked innocently.

"Wife!" Trimmer said, and began fanning herself vigorously. "What nonsense you speak, child. Wife indeed!''

"Oh, I assure you it is a possibility," Melora insisted. "A pity weddings aren't performed in the mosque. I should love to see inside one.''

Leitrim regarded her warily. "Would you also like to spend the rest of your days in Arabia?" he asked sardonically. "Rather confining for a lady who is accustomed to doing as she pleases.''

"Why, to tell the truth, as Rashid speaks English so fluently, I had some thoughts of taking him home each year for the Season.''

"We shall have to change your name to Lady Persephone," Leitrim smiled. "Zeus took pity on her when she was carried off by Pluto, and allowed her out of Hades annually for the Season. I trust you didn't eat anything while in the desert? It was the pomegranate seeds that did poor Persephone in.''

"I shouldn't call this castle Hades," Melora countered, looking around at the room's rich appointments.

"The mind is its own place—so Milton tells us. It can make a hell of heaven. Your mind is not the sort that will fit easily into the narrow confines of a lady's life here.''

"What do you know about my mind?" she demanded.

"What your behavior—or lack of it—has shown me. You don't love Rashid. You only want to show the world you can conquer him. It would amuse you to lead him about the polite salons of London on a leash. You won't find him a tame pet, milady."

"But what a swath we could cut in those polite salons."

"A wider swath than you know—you and his other three wives."

"Other wives!" she exclaimed.

"Did His Excellency not mention it, during your discussion of marriage? A good Muslim is permitted four wives, Melora. A new figure for marriage. The triangle we are familiar with, of course. You may be only one of Rashid's four wives, but the five of you will be the only marital pentagon in London."

She was shocked, but not about to let Leitrim see it. "It was only a preliminary discussion. Naturally I would not tolerate any other wives," she said calmly.

Trimmer was allowed to show all the shock she wanted. "Four wives! I never heard of such a thing! Why they're worse than the royal princes. How do four women manage to live together without strangling each other?"

"Each is permitted her own domicile, I believe," Leitrim explained. "Four identical little apartments on Berkeley Square, and a quarter of the *shaikh's* time. That would be your lot."

Melora stared coldly. "There are some husbands whose time a wife would be happy to have diluted,'' she said. ''Rashid, of course, is not of that kidney. If he insisted on having four wives, then I would insist on having four husbands.''

''But are there four such fools in the world?'' Leitrim asked.

''Please leave now, Leitrim,'' Melora said bluntly. ''I want to take a bath.''

''I shall visit Rashid. Will it be in order for me to offer him my congratulations, or—''

''Don't you dare mention such a thing!'' she warned.

At his jaunty, knowing laugh, Melora could control her temper no longer. She picked up a book and threw it at him.

Leitrim caught it and looked at the cover. ''Orphan of the Rhine,'' he read. ''I shall borrow this, Trimmer, if you don't mind. I may find a clue how to deal with the Orphan of the Thames.''

He bowed and left, smiling.

Chapter Eight

At nine the next morning, Melora heard a discreet tap at her apartment door. When she opened it, Leitrim stepped in. "Good morning," he said. He eyed her English gown askance. It was a fashionable sprigged muslin that looked very attractive, and was much too revealing for Arabia.

"Good morning."

"No complaints for me today? You've been immured for twelve hours. I made sure you'd be pining for the great outdoors by now."

"I'm a little tired after yesterday's ride."

"Ah! Then you aren't interested in making a tour of the market place."

Her fatigue dissipated with amazing celerity. "The *souk*? Oh, I should love it of all things, Leitrim. I'll just get Miss Trimmer, and put on my *burnous.*"

"*Burnous*?" he asked. "It's only a short ride. You can wear your habit."

Melora had learned her lesson. "The *burnous* would be more comfortable."

"But not half so attractive."

"No one will see me. No one who matters, I mean."

He gave her a disgruntled look. "You mean the *shaikh* won't be along. That's true, but *I* shall see you, and be seen. A gentleman on the strut likes his lady to be in the highest kick of fashion." Melora gave an insouciant toss of her shoulders. "I had planned to visit Captain Redding for lunch," he added.

"Oh! Well in that case—"

"Yes, I rather thought the presence of half a dozen handsome young officers might change your mind. They're all ineligible younger sons, milady."

"Aren't I fortunate I'm an only child, and inherited all the money in the family? Penniless gentlemen hold no terrors for me. I'll tell Trimmer to prepare."

Trimmer joined Leitrim and Melora went to put on her habit.

"Another outing," Miss Trimmer smiled. "We are becoming quite spoiled by so much attention."

"We can't let Shaikh Rashid carry the day. The honor of English manhood is at stake," Leitrim joked.

Trimmer had no acquaintance with levity. She considered his words and replied, "I cannot speak for Melora. She has a strange wayward streak that actually enjoys ploughing through a merciless desert, but for myself, I always prefer shopping to anything else.''

"She was impressed with yesterday's outing, was she?''

"She never stops talking about it. Queen of the Desert, you know. That suits her vanity. I took no pleasure in watching his falcons murder innocent bustards.''

In a short while, Melora joined them, wearing her habit. "Will Ayesha be accompanying Miss Trimmer in the carriage?'' she asked.

"She doesn't go into public—certainly not with a bunch of foreigners,'' Leitrim said.

Melora gave him a knowing look. "Pity.''

"I shan't mind jostling along behind you two in the gig,'' Miss Trimmer assured them. "It is quite comfortable, and the groom is well-behaved.''

"The horses are waiting. Shall we go?'' Leitrim said.

Shaikh Rashid's mounts and the carriage were waiting inside the castle walls. Melora rode Désirée again.

"I usually ride Sinbad,'' Leitrim said, patting a handsome gray mare.

The two mounts pranced in their eagerness for exercise. Melora stroked the animal's nose in greeting. "You're a beauty. Yes, you are,'' she cooed, as though to a baby. "Her name's Désirée,'' she mentioned to Leitrim.

"Mine's Mike.''

She lifted her head and gave him a startled glance. "Mike,'' she said, trying the name against his appearance. "How very—Irish.''

"So my Da thought when he gave me the

monicker. He'd have called me Patrick, but my
Uncle Mike had more money to leave. The
scoundrel spent every sou of it before he died. That
taught us the futility of counting on others to help
us. Need a hand up?''

Melora had found the mounting block and got
aboard by herself. ''I like to look after myself as
well,'' she said.

Leitrim spoke to Trimmer's driver and they all
left. As they passed through the castle walls,
Melora's attention was drawn first to the ocean,
that glowed like molten copper in the sun. The
white sails of dhows peacefully plied the waters.
Next she gazed around at the land. It lay flat in all
directions, a grayish-brown floor with some sparse
grass and a cluster of dispirited palm trees.

''The salt inhibits growth, here close to the sea,''
Leitrim explained.

''It's rather like our salt marshes at home.''

''We're heading east—this way,'' Leitrim told
her. ''The Arabians' preferred pace is a gallop.
We'll let them have a go to get rid of their jitters,
then come back and stay with Miss Trimmer.''

Melora urged her mount forward. They flew
along the sand, with the sea gleaming on their left.
The sands stretched endlessly beyond on the other
side. The Arabians kept a smooth pace as their
long legs flew like pistons, sure-footed, fast,
indomitable. Melora slowed to a trot when she
espied a caravan of camels coming toward them,
jogging along with a see-saw motion. Their legs
were so long and slender they looked like stilts, but
it was their faces that she stared at. Strange,
haughty faces they had.

''Will the men be hostile?'' she asked.

"Not overtly, at least. They'll recognize the mounts. Shaikh Rashid's guests aren't likely to be attacked."

The Arabs stared with such rampant curiosity that Melora drew back behind the concealment of Leitrim's shoulder when the group passed. The camels looked dispirited as they plodded wearily along, heavily laden with bags. One old Arab rode in front of the pack. He swayed to and fro with each step in a way that almost made Melora seasick. Others slogged along on foot, to save the camels an unnecessary burden.

Leitrim addressed the elder, mounted Arab. The man made a salaam and the caravan passed peacefully by. "They're delivering goods to the castle," he explained. "Our first stop is the *souk*. I thought you might like to see the open market. It's four or five miles further along. We'll take an hour there, and be at the shipyard in time for lunch."

They set a slow pace, to keep Miss Trimmer's gig in view. After a mile, Melora drew to a stop. "Why are there so many seagulls ahead?" she asked, pointing upward. Against the azure sky, the glisten of white wings wheeled and soared and swooped.

"It's a fishing village. We'll stop a moment if you like."

They soon reached a stretch of beach that was full of activity. Small rowing boats moved about the water, casting nets for fish. In the distance, white sails stood out against the blue sky and silver water, with sea birds swooping everywhere, to see what they could pirate.

"Seafood makes up a large part of the Arab's diet," Leitrim explained. "Those things hanging to dry are giant sea turtles. They don't eat pork, of course, and as grazing is poor, mutton and lamb are luxuries.''

"You don't have to tell me they're short on cows. I have tasted their goat's milk. Fish at least seems plentiful.''

A group of workers were filleting the catch and laying the silvery filets on boards to dry in the sun.

"What is that huge thing—some sort of trap?'' Melora asked. "It's big enough to hold a man!''

"They're fish pots, brought to this tribe for repair.''

As he spoke, a child darted inside to help his master attach the torn mesh.

"He looks like a giant bird in a cage. Poor thing—working so young, and on such a lovely day.''

"But then it's better than working in a mine or mill, as your English children do, isn't it?'' he asked sardonically.

"And what do the Irish children work at?''

"Growing 'taties and cabbage, or helping with the cattle. Seen enough? I know you ladies always like to go shopping.''

"I have no money!'' she exclaimed, aghast.

He gave her a quizzing smile. "Aren't you lucky I'm along? If you're very good, I might lend you a few *sheckles*.''

"If I have to repay it, I shouldn't have to be good too. What interest do you charge, usurer?''

"Only a hundred percent.''

"I've fallen into the hands of the cent per-centers!'' she laughed, and they returned to their mounts.

They continued on to the outdoor marketplace, that ran parallel to the beach in a little village. The scent of spices, perfume and incense wafted toward them as they advanced. Then the babble of foreign voices raised in haggling was heard. They dismounted at the edge of the market and began strolling with Miss Trimmer through the stalls. It was an exotic scene of noise and commotion. Blankets had been arranged on poles to protect the vendors from the sun. Colorful wares were spread out on tables below. In the shade of some stalls, elderly men were hunched over their cups. Some of them were smoking *hookahs.* Ephemeral white ropes of smoke curled above their heads, to dissipate in the breeze. Behind the bazaar, a crumbling mosque cast its shadow on the sand.

Melora darted to and fro like a child at a party.

"Oh look, what's this for, Leitrim?" she asked, lifting a brass samovar.

"It's for making tea."

"Shall we buy it, Miss Trimmer?"

"We have nine tea pots at home."

"But what a lovely conversation piece. Let's buy it."

Leitrim stepped forward and negotiated the bargain, then had to carry the samovar. "It would be more to the point to buy a gift for your host," he suggested.

"I hadn't thought of that!" Melora said. "Yes, we must buy something for Rashid."

"Rashid?" he asked, lifting a brow in disapproval. "I hadn't realized you were on a first name basis with His Excellency."

"Of course I don't call him that to his face, but yesterday he *did* call me Melora."

"I noticed you haven't taken my hint to call me Michael. Nor did I hear any invitation to drop the 'Lady' when speaking to yourself."

Melora's interest had wandered to the next stall, where a pretty casket of hammered brass had caught her attention. "How sweet. It looks like a little miniature coffin. What is it?"

At the word 'coffin' Miss Trimmer gave the box a horrified look and stepped away from it.

Leitrim flipped open the domed lid. "A lady's make-up casket," he said, and began lifting various items. "This is *kohl,*" he said, showing her a small black stick. "Ladies wear it to enhance their eyes. And this red powder is *alcanna*—we call it henna."

"For dying hair, you mean?"

Miss Trimmer leaned forward and peered into the box. "In the East they use it to dye parts of the body," Leitrim explained. "It comes from an Egyptian privet."

Miss Trimmer patted her gray hair and added the henna to the coffin.

"I shall use the chest to hold my perfumes and powder," Melora decided.

"We're buying it then, are we?" he asked.

"Yes, please. Ask him how much it costs?"

Leitrim spoke to the vendor, and a long haggle ensued. "Don't be so cheap, Michael," she scolded. "Pay him what he wants."

"This isn't the Pantheon Bazaar, my dear. I would offend the gentleman's dignity if I didn't drive a hard bargain. We're halfway there. You turn away as though you'd lost interest."

Melora and Miss Trimmer went along to the next stall, where Melora immediately fell in love with a hammered gold necklace, curiously wrought, and beaded with semi-precious stones.

She took it to Leitrim. "Never mind the casket! Look what I found! It will be marvelous with my masquerade costume."

"What masquerade costume?"

"The one I plan to wear when I reach London. I shall go as a Persian dancing girl."

"I've just beat the merchant down to a very good bargain on the casket."

"Excellent. We'll put the necklace in the casket for now. With room to spare, though I fear Trimmer's samovar won't quite fit."

"We can't carry so much."

"Why, your wits are gone begging," Miss Trimmer said. "You can put all the parcels in the gig with me."

"Of course," Leitrim agreed, juggling the wares. "Meanwhile I'll be mistaken for a merchant myself. Now what about a gift for our host—"

"Let us take another look at the gold and silver jewelry," Melora decided.

"We only want a token," he said. "I don't think jewelry fills the bill."

"True, I cannot hope to compete with that collection of diamonds and pearls Rashid has at the castle."

Melora spotted a small cloisonné box amidst the welter of bijoux and lifted it. "Oh look, Michael! A peacock. Doesn't it just remind you of the *shaikh*? I shall buy this. What is it for, headache powder?"

"Peacocks always give me the megrims," Miss Trimmer said. "It is their screeching that does it."

"It could be used for that," Leitrim said, and

opened the little box to examine it. "This will do fine. Now begins the bargaining."

The ladies continued to the next stall, and entered a little room to examine the silks. Miss Trimmer had her heart set on a patterned length for an evening shawl. After she had examined several pieces, Melora became bored and wandered to the doorway. Amidst the throng, she saw Monsieur Duval. He was talking to a man in a *burnous*. When Duval shifted his position, she recognized the young man.

"Trimmer! Look!" she exclaimed, and pointed to them. "It's the European prisoner who escaped from the Reliant!"

Duval looked up suddenly and spotted her. She waved and smiled to cover that she'd been spying. By the time Miss Trimmer got to the doorway, the young man had vanished in the throng. Melora ran to tell Leitrim. Watching her, Duval hastened forward and greeted the party.

"Who was that man you were talking to, Monsieur Duval?" Melora asked at once.

Leitrim gave a quelling stare, but she didn't see, or at least didn't heed it.

"No one you would like to know. I fear he is not a gentleman," Duval replied.

But she wanted to learn more about him, and pressed on. "As our European contingent here is so small, could we not call him one of the nonce and be presented to him?"

"Much good it would do. He speaks no English."

"Nous parlons français, monsieur."

"Malheureusement, Herr Gimmel speaks only German and *ein bisschen* of Arabic."

"He is German then?" Melora asked.

Duval hunched his shoulders. "So I assume. He might possibly be Dutch—the languages sound similar to me. I have hardly done more than nod to the fellow. How is the *shaikh* today?"

They chatted a moment before Leitrim suggested they be on their way. As soon as they were beyond earshot of Duval, he turned a wrathful eye on Melora.

"Why did you let him know you'd seen that man?"

"He knew I had seen him. He saw me staring at them together. It would have looked odd not to mention it. A white face stands out in this country. Naturally I would be curious."

"You're sure that's the fellow who was on the Reliant?"

"She doesn't make mistakes about men, Leitrim," Trimmer assured him.

"Then we have confirmation that Duval is in on the piracy," Leitrim said. "I was convinced already, but his being with that fellow proved it to my satisfaction."

"Duval could be telling the truth. I only saw them together for a moment," Melora told him.

Leitrim snorted. "A pity you alerted Duval that we're on to him."

"I didn't tell him I recognized the man."

"You shouldn't have mentioned him at all. You should have let on you didn't see him."

"He saw me looking at him. You always want to put me in the wrong."

"I would be extremely grateful if someone would put you in the right for once. Why did you have to wave to Duval in the first place?"

She was tired of defending her perfectly natural reaction and answered lightly, "A lady must flirt with someone, milord. How else am I to get in fighting trim for the Marriage Mart in London next Season?"

"I can't believe you'll have any trouble."

"Why thank you, I think—"

"A dowry of fifty thousand will always interest the gentlemen."

"I see you've gone to the trouble of ascertaining my value."

"But of course, Lady Melora. I might add it was very little trouble. The sum has been tossed in my direction more than once."

"Not with any intention of getting an offer from you."

"I have two younger, fairly penniless brothers I mean to put forward for your consideration."

"If they're anything like you, you need not bother."

"Oh they're not. We're talking tame pups here. You could bring them round your finger with no trouble. I rather think you would like them. For God's sake let us get away from this place."

"My silk!" Miss Trimmer exclaimed. "You must go into that little hut and haggle the man down to a bargain, Leitrim. I want a good, low price. A penny spent is a penny earned."

He sighed wearily and followed them into the stall. "I must have been mad to go shopping with two ladies."

"No more!" Leitrim begged, when he had completed the transaction and added the silk to his burdens. "We're due to meet Captain Redding very shortly. We must be on our way."

With a last, longing look at the bazaar, the ladies turned reluctantly away. "How much do I owe you?" Melora asked.

"You'll receive the reckoning when we get home."

"You didn't buy anything," she said, much struck with his forbearance. "Do you never cave in to the impulse of the moment, Michael?"

"Very rarely, which is fortunate for you," he said, frowning at the parcels which were proving cumbersome. But at length he had them arranged in Trimmer's carriage and they continued their journey.

Chapter Nine

"Where will we meet Captain Redding?" Melora asked as they continued their trip along the coast.

"At the dhow yard, but we'll be taking lunch at a little house John Company has leased nearby. Redding will be overseeing repairs to his Reliant."

Soon they came to the shipyard, where a few sailors in uniform were inspecting the work in progress. Other new dhows were in the process of being built. Arabs bent over the ships' skeletons, hammering, measuring, fitting pieces together like a jigsaw puzzle, as they had been doing from time immemorial.

"There's Redding now," Leitrim said, as he caught sight of the Captain pacing toward them.

"Ah, Leitrim! And ladies. I trust you and your chaperone are being well taken care of, Lady Melora?"

"We're treated like queens at Shaikh Rashid's castle, sir. The *shaikh* could not be kinder," Melora replied.

"It shan't be for much longer. They tell me here our Reliant will be seaworthy soon, then we shall be on our way home," Redding explained.

"There's no hurry," Melora said, with a peculiar little smile.

Redding gave a sharp, inquisitive look at the other captain, then smiled. "I daresay Leitrim is entertaining you."

"Only trying, Captain," Leitrim said. "It is the *shaikh* that is the real interest."

"He can be a good host, if he makes up his mind to it."

"Shall we go?" Melora asked. "I should like to get inside so I can remove this veil. It's like breathing through a bag."

Redding offered her his arm. "Right this way. My little cottage is comfortable enough."

Leitrim escorted Miss Trimmer to the little house built in the European style, but with a tiled roof and shutters against the sun. As the servants were junior seamen from the ship, the ladies were able to cast off their veils and breathe freely. Lunch was waiting for them, served at a table with chairs and all the usual conveniences. There was even cow's milk for tea, which pleased Miss Trimmer. The Captain had a humpbacked cow tethered in the yard. A few officers joined them for lunch.

"Are you making any progress convincing the *shaikh* to sign the truce?" Captain Redding asked.

"I dislike to make an open threat," Leitrim replied, frowning. "Rashid doesn't like to go to war with the Joasimees, but I don't think they're at the bottom of this rash of piracy. It's Rahma b. Jabir—with some help from the Frenchman.''

"It would help if we could discover where they hide out, and see for ourselves that it is Rahma b. Jabir Duval's using. If we could convince Rashid he need not fight the Joasimees, I think he'd sign. But how to find our way through the labyrinth of hills?''

"It isn't easy," Leitrim said. "Rashid's agreed to discuss the truce with the other *shaikhs* in the area. His sister is marrying Shaikh Murad, so that should ensure another important signature."

Melora gave a startled look. "You didn't tell me that, Michael!" She stared as a tinge of pink rose up his neck.

Leitrim cleared his throat. "I didn't realize you are interested in the details of the truce."

"I'm not, but I'm interested in your romance with Ayesha," she said.

"A private joke," Leitrim explained, stiff with embarrassment, and immediately changed the subject. "We have pretty good evidence Duval is involved in the piracy. Lady Melora spotted him with that European prisoner who jumped overboard the night you were attacked by pirates. He's been at the castle too, trying to ingratiate himself by turning into a scholar of the Koran.''

Redding shook his head. "Shaikh Rashid takes his religion seriously. Duval's a clever scoundrel. He'd use anyone, or anything." His eyes slid to Lady Melora as he spoke. She was talking to one of the junior officers.

"Yes," Leitrim agreed in a quiet aside. "The sooner we get the ladies bounced off, the better."

"Your term with the Marine is over soon,

Leitrim,'' Redding continued. "Have you decided whether you'll sign on for another stint?"

"I mean to stay till I succeed with Shaikh Rashid. I've spent considerable time getting to know him, and gain his trust. Another officer would have to start from scratch.''

"You must be eager to get home. Your father would be getting on by now. Your estate and people need you. Time you marry and settle down." Again his eyes slid to Melora, but he said nothing more.

Miss Trimmer turned to Redding and said, "I'm surprised you don't serve rum at your table, Captain. I had a taste of it the other day. A pleasant change from wine. Would it be possible for me to take home a bottle? I have a little trouble sleeping,'' she added. "It's better than laudanum.''

"I'm sure that could be arranged.''

"Just a small bottle,'' Leitrim said firmly. The gentlemen exchanged a meaningful look.

"I always find an inactive day keeps me awake,'' Redding commented. "Things are dull at the castle, I daresay.''

Melora blinked in surprise. "Dull? Oh no, they are fascinating! We went riding in the desert yesterday, and saw the *shaikh's* falcons.''

The officer beside her smiled. "I'm sure Shaikh Rashid finds life interesting, since your arrival, Lady Melora.''

She flushed in pleasure, and said, "I cannot complain of a lack of courtesy. He is a little pompous, you know, but I am quizzing him out of that.''

Redding stiffened up. "You must remember his

position, Lady Melora! To hear of your quizzing
him . . . He might take that amiss.''

"He doesn't seem to, does he, Leitrim?''

"He is always gallant with foreign visitors.''

Melora resumed her flirtation with the young
officer, and Redding spoke in a low voice to
Leitrim. "That one has a little more life than most
ladies, and her chaperone, you know, is next to
useless. We had a taste of Lady Melora's antics
aboard the Reliant. She talked the helmsman into
letting her take the wheel, and nearly ran us
aground. You won't let her run out of bounds, eh
lad? You could try your own hand at courting her,
if all else fails. She's extremely eligible, by the
way.''

"You need not worry she'll take the wheel while
I'm in charge, Captain.''

After lunch, the visitors made their adieux and
left.

They made no stops on the way home, but only
slowed down at the points of interest. As they
approached the castle, Melora drew her mount to a
halt and gazed at it. It rose like a gilded fairy castle
in the distance. The round turret was crenelated at
the top, with long, narrow windows. Open stone
work along the ramparts was furred with sunlight,
casting a golden glow over the whole.

"It's like a fairy castle,'' she sighed. "What
makes it glow so, Michael?''

"Probably the coral that's mixed with the clay.''

"And there's my balcony,'' she pointed out.
"Just like Juliet's. What a famous stage set it
would make.''

"Bear in mind the *shaikh* is no young Romeo.
Mind you,'' he added teasingly, "I have been

known to scale a castle wall before now."

"Indeed? I thought a Tar would be more accustomed to scaling masts and rigging."

"They are only practice for the more interesting climbs."

"Whose walls did you scale—or is it indiscreet of me to ask?"

"You know it is. And I, being the very soul of discretion, shall not satisfy your curiosity. But she was a charmer," he added mischievously.

She gave an unconcerned smile, but in her eyes, a glint of interest appeared. "I didn't think you would go to so much trouble to seduce an antidote," she said, and nudged her mount into motion.

They left their mounts with servants inside the walls and went with Miss Trimmer to the carved door of the castle. The *shaikh* was pacing the hallway. His bronze skin and dark eyes stood out dramatically against the startling white of his *burnous*. He rushed forward to greet Melora, seized her hand and raised it to his lips.

"I shall give thanks to Allah for your safc return. You must join me for tea. Miss Trimmer agrees?" His face glowed with pleasure as he studied her eyes, that sparkled alluringly behind her veil. Soon he would see the whole, enchanting face.

"Thank you, Your Excellency. I am delighted, but first I must make a fresh toilette. I have bought you a gift," she added.

"This is not necessary, milady. Your presence is all the gift I desire."

Leitrim put a hand on her elbow. "We'll be down presently, Your Excellency," he said, and drew Melora away.

As they mounted the stairs, she said triumphantly, "He was waiting for me."

"Such transparent glee at your conquest is hardly becoming. One would think him your first beau."

"Hardly that—but he is the most fascinating," she replied with a saucy smile. "Give me my parcels, Leitrim."

At the doorway, he gave her the items purchased at the bazaar, and went to his room to freshen up. Trimmer was intrigued with her samovar. "I wouldn't have a notion how to use it, but for now I shall pour my rum into it. It seems so shabby to have the bottle sitting about." She poured a tot into a glass and drank thirstily. "Driving always raises a thirst."

"We'll be having tea soon," Melora said, and took out the *shaikh's* little box to smile at it.

"We should have got something for Leitrim," Miss Trimmer said.

"Leitrim?" Melora looked surprised. "Why should I buy him a gift?"

"He saved our lives. How very like you to omit the one indispensable gift."

"I could hardly buy him a gift with his own money."

"Always handy with an excuse when you know you've behaved badly," Trimmer scolded.

A knock at the door interrupted their conversation. It was Ayesha, carrying a blue silk robe, which she handed to Melora. "For lady. From *shaikh*," she said, and immediately left.

Melora stared at it, fingering the fine silk. "Look at this, Miss Trimmer. A gift from Rashid.

I shall put it on at once." She whirled into her bedroom and began changing.

In his room, Leitrim did no more than wash the dust of travel from his hands and face, brush his hair, and put on a new cravat. He was back at the ladies' door within minutes, to be told Lady Melora was changing her clothes.

"The *shaikh* is waiting!" Leitrim exclaimed. "One does not keep His Excellency waiting. Tell her to hurry up."

"She's changing," Miss Trimmer told him, and closed the door.

Leitrim began pacing the hallway. He glanced at his watch. After five lengths of the hall, he drew it out again. After another five, he rapped sharply at the door once more.

"She's nearly ready," Trimmer assured him.

More pacing, more knocking. The hand of his watch crept from three-thirty to four, and still the wretched girl didn't come. At four o'clock he could stand no more, and went charging into the room, just as Melora was putting the finishing touches to her coiffure.

"We are ready, Michael," she said demurely.

Leitrim stared at the transformation. She was dressed in the blue silk caftan, that fell in graceful folds from her shoulders to the floor, where a gold key pattern edged the hem. The bodice plunged daringly low, to reveal the rise of creamy bosoms. The deep sapphire tones of the gown matched her eyes perfectly. She raised an arm, and the wide sleeve fell like another skirt. At her feet, dainty gold sandals peeped out.

"Where did you get that?" he demanded.

"A present from His Excellency. He had it made

up as a surprise during my absence. Very thoughtful, is he not? The shade is a perfect match for my eyes.''

Leitrim's jaw muscle quivered with the effort to contain his wrath. ''Such thoughtfulness deserves a better reward than an hour's wait.''

''Not that long, surely! I couldn't go to meet him all covered in dust. I'm so glad you reminded me to buy him a token. I should have bought more than that little box, I fear.''

''Come along,'' Leitrim said gruffly, and they left.

Lady Melora ignored the veil Trimmer handed her and walked downstairs with her face bare and her head high. Fortunately, she didn't meet anyone. She looked like an empress, and felt like one.

The *shaikh* broke with tradition and was awaiting his guests when they joined him in the European Salon. His eyes turned at once to Melora; his expression softened to what any fool could see was love.

''Your Excellency,'' Melora smiled, and made a dainty curtsey before going forward to take his hand. ''Pray forgive my tardiness. I didn't want to come to you in the dust of travel. Such a lovely gift as this gown deserves my best effort. Thank you so much.''

He batted the apology aside. ''My patience is well repaid. *Ravissante*, my dear.''

Melora flickered a triumphant smile at Leitrim and took up a seat behind the tea pot. Flushed with victory, she pushed her luck a little further.

''We had lunch with Captain Redding, sir,'' she smiled at Rashid. ''You'll never guess what he has.

He has found a cow. It was so pleasant to have real milk for one's tea." She filled the cups and passed the first one to the *shaikh*.

Shaikh Rashid lifted the creamer and poured milk into her cup. "Drink it," he said, gazing into her eyes.

"You know I detest goat's milk!"

"Drink it," he repeated firmly.

The haughty tilt of his chin set nerves on edge. The guests exchanged an uncomfortable frown, wondering what would come next. Melora looked at Leitrim. He nodded his head vigorously. She lifted the demi tasse and sipped diffidently. Then a smile broke. "Rashid! How did you . . . It's real milk, Trimmer!"

The tension broke and Trimmer eagerly took hold of the creamer. "So very thoughtful of you, Your Excellency. How did you manage it?"

Rashid reluctantly withdrew his gaze from Melora and said to Trimmer, "When the *shaikh* commands, his people obey. The cow was brought from the closest village this morning. You too must call me Rashid, Trimmer. As your charge has done me the honor of using my short name, I may take the same privilege with her—yes?"

Melora lifted her fingers to her lips. "I'm sorry, Your Excellency! It just slipped out in the excitement of the moment."

"I am honored, I assure you, Melora," Rashid smiled. His accents were soft. The name was drawn out—liquid, flowing.

Leitrim sat unnoticed, his knuckles turning white as he gripped his tea cup. To break the strangely seductive mood that was creeping over the tea party, he spoke in a hearty, mundane way.

"I took the ladies to the *souk*, and to see the fishermen. They enjoyed the open market—bargains galore."

"It beats the London shops," Melora added. "Of course Leitrim, being a man, wouldn't linger long enough for anything. I didn't even get to buy any silk."

"My people have all manner of silk here at the castle," the *shaikh* assured her. "You must feel free to make use of what you desire. They are excellent needlewomen. The fit was all that was missing, which is why your gown is loose. Also, it is cool for our climate. Binding gowns, though attractive, retain the heat."

"Oh, it's lovely," Melora assured him. "I fear my little token gift is quite cast into the shade, Rashid. I shall do better before I leave. Meanwhile, I bought this for you," she said, and handed him the little cloisonné box.

The *shaikh* accepted it, held it in his fingers, fondling it, admiring the trifle as though it were a diamond. "You find me vain, like the peacock?" he teased, but in good humor.

"The peacock has cause for his vanity. He is the most beautiful bird we have at home," she told him.

He acknowledged the compliment with a nod. He flipped open the lid and gazed inside the box.

"It is to hold headache powders—or something," Melora explained.

"For when the peacocks' screeching gives you a headache," Miss Trimmer added, nodding wisely.

Rashid looked disappointed. "I had hoped for a lock of your hair inside," he said simply.

"Oh!" Melora looked uncertainly at Trimmer

and Leitrim, who looked back at her in the same way. "I shall be happy to give you one," she said.

The *shaikh* snapped his fingers. A servant was sent for scissors, and he examined Melora's coiffure. "Not one that will be missed," he said, using it as an excuse to touch her curls. His fingers brushed her neck gently, with a warm touch.

Uncomfortable, Melora laughed. "It's like Pope's *Rape of the Lock*. 'The meeting points the sacred hair dissever/From the fair head, forever, and forever.' "

The scissors snipped, and a golden curl was twined around the *shaikh's* tanned finger. He lifted it away and smiled at it. "Rape is not what I have in mind, Melora. Only a souvenir. I shall have a noble memory, as your Shakespeare says." He placed the curl in the box carefully, snapped the lid and hid the box in the recesses of his *burnous*.

"I have set tomorrow aside for you," he said to Melora. "Today was Lord Leitrim's turn. Tomorrow, I teach you to ride a camel. It is an indispensable skill for a lady living in my country."

Leitrim stirred restively, but Melora wasn't looking at him. "I should love to try it!" she said.

"We shall visit my friend, Shaikh Ali Murad." He turned aside to include Leitrim in the conversation. "Also, I shall speak to him about that business matter, milord."

Leitrim used it as an excuse to include himself in the outing. "Perhaps I should go with you."

The *shaikh*, serene in his authority, just shook his head and said nothing. When the tea was finished, he rose with Leitrim and bowed to the ladies.

"We shall stop by your room this evening to

wish you good night," he promised.

"This time, I hope you will come in," Melora said. With a long, inviting glance, she curtsied and left.

Leitrim hurried after her. "This thing is getting out of hand. I don't like his calling you a lady who is 'living' in the desert. You're just a visitor."

"But I most especially want to ride a camel. When the *shaikh* commands, his subjects obey," she laughed. "One of these days the *shaikh* will obey too. I still mean to visit a mosque."

"We are not his subjects! I won't watch you flirting with him in this insupportable manner. It's outrageous!"

"Then don't come to say goodnight this evening."

"Trimmer!" Leitrim said helplessly.

"Don't be such a gudgeon, Michael," Melora scolded. "Everything is open and public. He is only playing the gallant. What harm does it do if he wants a lock of my hair?"

"Do you really think he's going to be satisfied with a lock of your hair, when you incite him with every glance?"

"It's all I plan to give him—for the present," she said saucily.

They had reached the ladies' apartment. Leitrim left them at the door. Melora went in first, wearing a satisfied smile.

"What do you think, Trimmer?" she asked. "Do you think the *shaikh* has designs on my virtue?"

"Pshaw. He is a real gentleman. Imagine finding a cow for me, in this barren place. I must get busy on the *shaikh's* tea cosy to repay him.'' She took up the knitting and began working on it.

"Michael seems to think he could be dangerous.''

"Leitrim is in a bad skin because of Ayesha marrying that Shaikh Murad. One cannot help but feel sorry for him. He is so dreadfully in love with her.''

"In love with Ayesha? No, it is just a passing fancy, surely. He cannot love her.''

"How blind the young are,'' Trimmer said, shaking her head. "Have you not seen him follow her with his eyes when she is in the room? He cannot get his fill of gazing at her. Mind you, she is very graceful in all her movements—quite a mystery lady.''

Lady Melora's pretty face wore very definite signs of pique at hearing this speech. "She's probably gaptoothed,'' she said angrily.

Miss Trimmer lowered her head over her knitting and smiled contentedly. That had got the chit thinking!

Chapter Ten

Miss Trimmer sat knitting the tea cosy while Lady Melora filed her nails. "Do you really think Michael's in love with Ayesha?" Melora asked.

"Oh my dear, as plain as the nose on your face. He is utterly captivated. She is so shy and sweet. Men like that."

"Rashid doesn't." Melora picked up her riding hat and tilted it rakishly over one eye. "Shall I wear this tomorrow to ride the camels, Trimmer?"

"Hush, I'm casting off stitches for the spout. Now you've made me lose count," she complained, then looked up. "It would look very strange with the veil you shall have to wear."

"I hate veils. Oh, there he is now," she said, as a knock sounded at the door.

"Take the knitting!" Trimmer said, and handed it to Melora before admitting the gentlemen.

When they were all seated, Shaikh Rashid said,

"Tonight Lord Leitrim is our host. He has had claret sent over from his English Captain friend. It will be brought presently."

His eyes were never long away from Melora, as she made some desultory and uncertain motions with the needles. "What is that craft you are performing?" he asked.

"It's the tea cosy I promised you, sir. See the progress I have made." She held it up for his examination.

Rashid took the knitting and studied it. "You make a very fine stitch, Melora."

"Excellent progress, considering—" Leitrim said ironically.

She gave him a baleful stare. "Considering what?" she demanded. "I have been working for several hours."

"This is very boring for you," Rashid said, setting the knitting aside. "We must provide better entertainment for the ladies, Lord Leitrim. I shall have a party. You will invite the Captain who sent us the wine, and some of his officers. I shall ask a few European friends as well. Say—dinner and music? You will make the invitations in my name and see when the guests can come. Make it next week. I must be away for a few days arranging Ayshea's marriage portion."

Melora turned and studied Leitrim. "Certainly, Your Excellency," he said. His voice didn't sound strained, but she imagined his cheeks turned a little pale.

The wine was delivered and served by Ayesha's female servants, who cast enticing eyes at their master. Watching him, Melora noticed the *shaikh's* interest in their allurements. He gazed blatantly at the women's bodies, and smiled a lazy smile as one beauty placed a glass before him. He was a sensual man, easily aroused to passion. The first stirring of jealousy struck her, and she moved to get his attention back.

"You have very pretty servants, Rashid," she said.

"These are my sisters' servants. Ayesha felt you would be more comfortable being served by women. I have men servants."

"That is very thoughtful of her," Miss Trimmer said.

"She is a model of kindness. Murad's family are fortunate to be getting her."

"Does she love Shaikh Murad?" Melora asked.

Rashid shrugged his shoulders. "It is a good marriage. Love may come, in time."

"Let us propose a toast to the couple. You must make the toast, Rashid," she demanded.

He lifted his glass. "To the wedding." They all drank. "And another toast to my honored English guests," Rashid said, and drank alone.

Melora looked at the others and said, "We must reciprocate. To our honored host," She lifted her glass, gazing at him over the rim as she drank.

"My, it's warm in here, isn't it?" Trimmer commented, and picked up a fan to create a breeze.

"It is because you keep your door closed, ladies. The wind tower catches the cool evening breeze and circulates it through the castle. Perhaps you could leave the door open during the day," the *shaikh* suggested.

Leitrim rose and opened the balcony door.

"Where is the wind tower?" Melora asked.

"Would you care to see it?" the *shaikh* asked at once.

"Yes, I should like to tour the whole castle some time. I was just remarking to Leitrim today it looks like a romantic fairy palace, all glowing in the sunlight. How fortunate you are to live here."

"By moonlight, it is even more romantic," he replied, and rose to offer her his hand.

"You're not going now!" Trimmer exclaimed.

Leitrim hopped to his feet. "You are the one who complained of the heat, Miss Trimmer. We shall go along too."

"Trimmer is not finished her wine," Melora pointed out.

"It's cool enough now, with the balcony door open," Trimmer said, and made no move to rise.

"You will bear Miss Trimmer company during our absence," the *shaikh* said, rather imperatively, to Leitrim. Then he took Melora's elbow and led her from the room.

Leitrim watched helplessly as they walked away. "This isn't a good idea, to leave them alone together," he warned Trimmer.

"Good gracious, they're only going to the wind tower for a breath of fresh air. It's not as though they are eloping."

"There's plenty of fresh air here. The wind tower is at the other end of the castle."

"They were virtually alone in the desert for hours. What harm can a little stroll do tonight? Melora doesn't like too short a leash, Leitrim. She's like a hound I once had. Tie him up and he immediately gnawed his way through the rope. Let him roam a little, and he never came to harm. She's a sensible girl, beneath all her high spirits. Half the reason she is leading the *shaikh* on is to pester you. You make it too obvious you dislike it. *Why* you dislike it, however, is not so clear?" she added, and looked with sharp eyes for his answer.

"I'm responsible for her safety."

"Yes," she said thoughtfully. "You don't really think the *shaikh* would try anything? He's a gentleman after all, even if he ain't one of our own. Surely her position is all the protection she requires."

"I expect *he'll* behave—but will *she*?"

Trimmer considered this a moment. "You know where this wind tower is?"

"Of course. A highly romantic spot."

"Then perhaps you ought to tag along. You can keep an eye on her from a distance."

It was all the encouragement Leitrim needed. He hastened out the door and Trimmer took up the tea cosy to resume her knitting. She was well pleased with her handling of the romance that was slow to blossom, and her sly smile showed it.

Leitrim hastened along the dim corridors, up the stairs to the wind tower. At the top of the stairs, he saw the couple, their silhouettes etched in moonlight against the tower walls. The *shaikh's* white *burnous* stood out, a solid figure beside the more evanescent blue of Melora's gown. The breeze lifted her hair and stirred her skirts. She turned and gazed up at Shaikh Rashid.

"The breeze is delightful. You can see the ocean from here," she murmured. "Doesn't it look like quicksilver, with the moon playing over its surface?"

"I can see the ocean any night. It is for only a brief span I may see you." His voice was softly seductive. "Your eyes are like stars, Melora." Her name hung on the air, as he drew it out—Melooora.

Watching, Leitrim saw the white shadow of Rashid's arm move around her waist, and his shoulders tensed to alertness.

"It is, as the French say, *comme il faut* for us to be here alone?" Rashid asked.

"*Absolument*," she declared. "I trust you don't plan to assault me, Your Excellency?" Yet some sprout of caution urged her to use the formal title.

"That is a hard word, assault."

His tone was insinuating. Melora decided it was time to return the conversation to propriety. "You speak English very well—and some French too. Where did you learn languages?"

"I had a French *khoja*, when I was a boy. A—professor?"

"Tutor, perhaps."

"My French is better than my English, actually. You have no curiosity to learn my language?"

"It hardly seems worthwhile, when I shall be leaving so soon."

"Must you leave—so soon?" he asked. His hand closed over hers.

Leitrim's body lurched forward, but his feet remained rooted to the top step. He waited, listening anxiously, for Melora's reply.

"The ship will be repaired soon," she told him, but her voice was full of regret.

"There will be other ships. Stay a little longer, Melora. There is much I wish to show you."

"I'm not sure I can. You must show me the things that are important to you now—in the few days we have together."

His fingers slid up her arm. She lifted her head and looked a question at him. "All that is important to me is here," he said softly. "You have only to look in your mirror. I feel the peace of *fana* in your presence, and a terrible unease when we are apart. All day I paced the castle like a caged animal, wondering if you were safe . . . *Nom d'un nom*, I speak like a schoolboy," he said with a violent shake of his head. "You bewitch me, with your blue eyes."

His head descended and she felt the touch of his lips against her eyelids. The warm breeze stirred his robes, sending an aroma of spice into the air. He moved his head and gazed at her. His eyes were a black dazzle as his head descended, and his arms folded around her.

As their lips touched, Leitrim came hurtling forward, and they jumped apart.

"What is it? What's the matter?" Melora exclaimed.

Feeling a perfect fool, Leitrim said, "It's—it's Trimmer. She has one of her megrims, Lady Melora. You have her headache powders, I think?"

Melora gave him a long, scalding look, but didn't contradict him in front of the *shaikh*. "Yes, I'll get them. Excuse me, Rashid."

She strode angrily past Leitrim, twitching her skirts as she went. The *shaikh* remained a pace behind. "That megrim was unnecessary, Lord Leitrim. I am not a savage after all."

"You have plenty of women here," Leitrim said baldly. "Why must you go after her?"

"I don't have another like that one," the *shaikh* replied, and laughed. "There is not such another in all the corners of Arabia."

He left Leitrim at the corner. "You will say goodnight to the ladies for me. Good night, Lord Watchdog." With a little sneering laugh, the *shaikh* returned to his own quarters.

Leitrim closed the door firmly behind him when he went to the ladies' apartment. "This is it," he said angrily. "If you can't behave for five minutes alone with the *shaikh*, you're not going camel riding with him tomorrow."

Melora tossed her head and sniffed. "Try if you can stop me!"

"If necessary I'll put you back on the Reliant and lock you in your cabin."

"You're very fierce—with a lady," she taunted. "Take your threats and menaces to the *shaikh*. He'll be very disappointed if you try to stop the outing. I shouldn't be at all surprised if you aren't the one who finds himself locked up—without your precious truce. These supreme rulers are so high-handed. Nearly as bad as petty sea officers, who think because they can make a squad of seamen jump through hoops, they can rule the rest of us."

"By God, I didn't ask for the torture of having to play watch dog to a spoiled brat. The job was thrust on me against my will."

"Oh come now, Leitrim. You exaggerate. We are not all so passive as you in our romances. This is pique because you've let Ayesha slip through your fingers."

"This has nothing to do with Ayesha."

"The devil it hasn't! Don't think to take your anger out on me. Why don't you go after her, if she's what you want?"

Melora didn't wait for a reply, but flounced into her bed chamber and slammed the door. Leitrim clenched his jaw and looked at Trimmer.

"Now where did she get the foolish idea that I'm in love with Ayesha?"

"Aren't you—a little?"

"No, I'm fascinated a little perhaps, but I know there can be nothing for me there. And there can be nothing for Melora with Rashid."

"Give her a little longer leash, Leitrim," the dame suggested.

"What time are they going camel riding tomorrow?"

"Around eleven, I believe she mentioned."

Leitrim drew out his watch and glanced at it. "If I left right now, I'd be back by morning."

Trimmer looked at him in surprise. "Where are you going at this hour of the night? It's pitch black outside."

"Pitch black is the best time for spying."

"But where are you going, Leitrim? You cannot leave us alone—"

"No one will know I'm gone. I have to discover what Duval's up to—how many ships he has, where—whether he's working with the Joasimee's. . . . The coast at Raz-al-Khaimah is a rabbit warren. If I could discover his lair, we could block him—or even better, blow his dhows out of the water."

Trimmer's hand clutched her heart. "What if something happens to you?"

"In that unlikely event, you must get word to Captain Redding at once. Shaikh Rashid will take care of it."

"Oh I wish you would not go!"

"I wish I didn't have to. But I shan't take any foolish chances, Trimmer." He cast a frustrated glance at Melora's closed door. "Take care of the hellion," he said grimly, and left.

In his room he changed from his uniform to a black *burnous*. With the headdress knotted tightly and only his weathered face showing, he might pass for an Arab, if one didn't look too closely. When he was dressed, he stuck a pistol in his pocket and drew a knotted rope out from behind the bed. It was tethered to the bed. He threw it out the window and proceeded to climb down, bracing his toes against the castle wall and using the knots to break his fall. The scrambling black figure was clearly outlined in the moonlight, but once Leitrim was on the ground, he disappeared in shadows. Within minutes, he was mounted on one of Shaikh Rashid's prime Arabians, dashing through the night.

The coast by moonlight had a pale, serene beauty unlike that of daytime. Black silhouettes of palm trees and an occasional hut stood out against the white sand, and beyond, a gibbous moon reflected its light in the water. Leitrim looked over his shoulder and peered into the shadows as he galloped along, splashing through puddles as he went. The small fishing ships stood at rest now, bobbing peacefully in the sea. On he rode, enjoying Sinbad's steady gait, the feeling of animal strength, the breeze against his brow.

When he came to the foothills of the Marble

Mountains, he tethered Sinbad to a date tree. Concealed in the shadows, he emitted three low, trilling whistles. He waited. Whistled again. After three whistles, a ragged young boy of twelve or thirteen appeared before him. In his hand he carried a shepherd's staff.

"This way, sir," the boy said, in his own native tongue.

Leitrim was learning Arabic and switched to that language. "Have you seen the white-faced foreigner come this way?"

"Two gentlemen, sir. They ride on their horses into the mountains."

"Two of them?"

"One young, one older."

"That'd be Mónsieur Duval and his compatriot, Herr Gimmel. Did they go to the Joasimee's camp?"

"Oh no, sir. They go to visit Rahma b. Jabir. I know him by sight. A fierce pirate."

"You're certain of that?"

"Yes, sir."

"I thought so!"

They skirted around the flock of sleeping sheep, huddled like large boulders at the edge of the foothills. Before them lay the outline of the Al Hajar mountains, that rose not in peaks but in rough, ragged, rounded and undulating humps. The presence of more than a hundred kinds of marble caused the mountains to gleam in the moonlight—beautiful but menacing. And somewhere amidst the crevices, in the *wadis* and oases that comprised the range, Duval had ensconced himself to lead his band of pirates.

The passage was rough underfoot. Worse, it was

noisy. They didn't scale the mountains, but worked their way through twisting paths that were impossible to keep track of. The guide pointed out landmarks as he went, but Leitrim found the best he could do was to mark their general direction, heading to the right, with one peak higher than the rest serving as his compass. After perhaps an hour's travel, the guide stopped and pointed to a hump of rock more or less the size of St. Paul's Cathedral.

"There, behind this hump lies a *wadi* with a clean stream and a ravine, lined with palms," the boy said. "In the village there, the foreigner has a big house, and nearby are the homes of his fishermen."

Leitrim edged forward, peered around the corner and saw the glint of a sword propped on a guard's arm. The man's head hung forward, his eyes closed. Over the man's shoulder, Leitrim saw the rambling hulk of Duval's house.

He silently returned to his guide. "The ships," he said, "where are they anchored?"

The guide pointed to the left. "In an inlet below. The mountain falls to the sea in steps."

"I must see how many he has."

"It is dangerous, sir. There are guards all along the ridge."

Leitrim looked at his black garment, almost invisible even at this close range. "You stay here. I'll risk it." He gathered dirt in his hands and smeared his face, to hide his white skin. He removed his boots and socks and handed them to the guide. When this was done, he edged carefully forward, picking his way over the rough surface till he found a pass wide enough to allow him to slip through. He came suddenly to the precipice and gazed below at a flotilla of fifty or sixty dhows, gliding peacefully at anchor in the water.

He gazed out to sea, trying to get a bearing, for the fleet was fairly impregnable by land. An island lay not a mile away. "Abu Musa," he murmured. "About ten degrees west, I'd say. The longest finger inlet." A triumphant smile lifted his lips and he turned quickly back to join his guide.

The boy stood smiling at the ground. Looking down, Leitrim saw he had put on the boots. The boy took a step forward and tripped. As he went sprawling, he let out a shout of surprise, or pain.

Almost instantly the sound of running footsteps came from the direction of Duval's quarters. Leitrim grabbed the boy and held him motionless against the edge of the mountain, just as a shot whizzed past their heads. Another guard came, a few remarks were exchanged between the two men. Then they began advancing into the passage, rifles raised, looking all around.

Leitrim felt the boy tremble, and feared he'd shout out. He clamped his fingers over the boy's mouth and held him flat against the wall.

"It came from over there," one of the guards whispered, and began coming slowly toward them. He moved carefully, looking all around.

Leitrim tried to remain motionless, but he felt something slither over his bare foot, and glanced down. A snake, disturbed by the intruders, had awakened and gone looking for food. A python? It was large enough. Not venomous at least—it killed its prey by constricting and crushing. The snake curled itself around Leitrim's ankle. Perspiration beaded his brow as he fought back the instinct to escape.

The second guard began following in the footsteps of the first, slowly, cautiously advancing.

The snake couldn't be a python—the coloring was wrong. What could it be? Not a cobra—the head was too small. Should he try to shake it off—or would that excite it into biting? Why had he taken off his boots? The perspiration beaded and began sliding down his forehead. Leitrim clenched his jaws and, by a superhuman effort, remained perfectly rigid. The snake began lifting its head. Oh God, was it preparing to strike? The head swerved and the snake moved across to his other foot. And still the guards were coming, slowly, looking all around. It was over—if the snake didn't get him, the guards would.

Leitrim heard the sound of a rock overturning and closed his eyes to utter a last prayer. "Baaaaa. Baaaaa!" He opened his eyes. A wooly lost lamb was straggling along the path.

The guards laughed and grabbed it around the neck. One of them put it under his arm. "Tomorrow we have meat for dinner!"

Leitrim's guide gave a start of anger. Leitrim tightened his fingers over the boy's mouth till the guards had left. "Not a word," he whispered. He released the boy and looked down at the snake.

"Is it a dangerous kind?" he asked.

The boy looked and his eyes grew. "A krait! Very venomous! See the black stripes." He looked around for a rock to kill it.

The snake slithered over Leitrim's foot and disappeared. "Pity," the boy said. "You can get a jug of wine for a krait skin. Now we rescue my lamb, please?"

Leitrim handed him a gold coin. "Buy another."

A mischievous smile split the boy's face. "But she is my favorite, sir."

Leitrim dropped another coin in the outstretched palm.

"Her wool is of the finest, and besides, the meat of that particular kind—"

Leitrim gave him a suspicious frown. "She was very small. I'll give you another shilling."

"Please, sir. The boots instead. My father would be very proud to have such fine boots. He is going to Mecca next year. A long trip, and on foot."

Leitrim tousled the boy's curls and laughed. "Keep them then, baggage. You've earned them, but I doubt they'll ever see Mecca. A jug of wine is more like it."

"Oh, no sir! Six jugs at least."

"Six? You deserve a baker's dozen. You're a brave boy."

Leitrim dropped another gold coin into the boy's hand and they returned to the foothills.

Chapter Eleven

The camel ride was a disappointment. It was executed with all due pomp and ceremony, as all Rashid's entertainments were. Half a dozen of his men brought half a dozen camels, but Melora knew without asking which was to be hers. It was smaller than the others, and wore a shining new blanket over the hump.

"I wish I had such eyelashes!" was Miss Trimmer's exclamation when she was urged forward to examine the animal.

"They have two rows, for protection against the sand," Rashid explained. "The camel is called the ship of the desert, but the staff of life would be closer to it. Not only a beast of burden, it provides us milk, meat, fur, hide and companionship. I have been in the desert for over two weeks at a stretch. My camels survived on such sparse grass and scrub as they could find, with no water."

He assisted Melora onto the camel's back as he spoke. When the animal stood, she felt as though she were sitting on top of a roof. But the gait, once it got moving, was not frighteningly fast. Quite the contrary.

"Can't it go any faster?" she called down, as she walked up and down the beach, with a groom holding the line. The camel's large, padded feet fell with an audible plop at every step.

The camel was urged on to a faster pace, which proved so bumpy she soon clambered down.

"The poor things have no notion how to run," Miss Trimmer told her. "They put both legs on the one side forward at the same time."

Melora rubbed her backside and said, "That explains it!"

Riding Désirée was much more enjoyable, especially when she and Michael could escape without any attendants or grooms and canter over the beach in the cool light of morning. The sunrises were beautiful. They painted the sky in luminous puffs of peach and saffron and amethyst, and reflected their dazzling brilliance from the ocean. Some mornings they rode as far as the village, splashing through glistening pools of water caught in the sand.

They stopped at the edge of the village one morning to catch their breath. Melora gazed at the mosque. She still hadn't managed to get inside one.

"Everything here looks so old, doesn't it, Michael? At home we think the Tower of London or a Norman church is old, but here the buildings look blasted with antiquity. They must be thousands of years old."

"Hardly that ancient. Before Mohammed, they had nothing you could really call architecture. This building probably dates from the six or seven hundreds."

"That's pretty old. It's a shame Ayesha can't be married in the mosque." She cast a surreptitious glance at Leitrim. "She is marrying Murad tomorrow, you know."

"I know," he answered, with no visible emotion.

"Do you mind very much?"

"I'm very happy. It will encourage Murad to join Rashid in signing the truce."

"Oh Michael! I'm not talking about that. I mean are you hurt to be losing her?"

"She was never mine to lose, Melora." He finally looked her in the eye, and she could study him for signs of pain. She thought he looked wistful. "It was like one of those romances from chivalry, where the lady is high on a pedestal, with the knight looking up from below."

"If you love her, I think you should have at least made an effort to win her."

"Perhaps I would have, if something else hadn't come along."

"The truce again," she scoffed.

"I didn't mean that."

She looked with bright interest. "What did you mean?"

"Oh, just a touch of reality from the real world, to distract me from my romantical brooding," he said. A soft smile lifted her lips as they gazed at each other. "I mean Miss Trimmer, of course," he added.

"Of course."

"I wish Rashid hadn't invited us to attend the wedding reception."

"I'm thrilled to death to be going. Trimmer and I are eager to see the bridegroom."

The castle was bustling with activity during the remainder of the day. Ayesha's goods and servants would remove with her to her husband's home. Melora was dying of curiosity to know what else was going on behind the closed doors of the bride's quarters.

On the appointed afternoon, she and Miss Trimmer went in their best gowns to attend the wedding. Michael was there too, in his naval officer's uniform, looking so handsome Melora was sure the bride must be crying behind her veil. Her husband was not nearly as attractive. He was an older gentleman, portly, though apparently very wealthy. All his attendants looked prosperous.

The actual ceremony was brief and incomprehensible and not very interesting. Ayesha wore a colored gown, in lieu of the dark ones usually worn. She was quiet, apparently serene, though of course no one could see her face. There was a holy man there, who said a few words. The groom didn't kiss the bride, but just took her hand possessively in his. The reception after the wedding was the more interesting occasion. It seemed the whole village had gathered for the party.

Rashid had whole lambs roasted over an open spit. There were baskets of melons, pomegranates, grapes and figs, and trays of sweets. The guests were served drinks while the entertainment went forth. Musicians played eerie, discordant music on peculiar instruments—long horns and stringed instruments, while the entertainers danced. There were no seductive dancing *houris*, but men, who used swords as part of the ritual.

Ayesha sat with her husband's party, watching. While Rashid circulated amidst the party, the English guests sat together.

"Not exactly as we would do it at St. George's in Hanover Square," Miss Trimmer said quietly. "This is more like a show than anything else. And the bride isn't even the star. Do you suppose Ayesha actually cares for that fat old man she is marrying?"

Gazing across the throng to Ayesha, Leitrim said, "Rashid says she is more than agreeable to the match."

"I hope it may be true," Trimmer said doubtfully. "Where there is marriage without love, you know—"

"There will be no love without marriage here," he said. "Death by stoning is the married adulterer's lot. The unmarried get away with a hundred lashes."

"Does the bridegroom have other wives?" Melora asked.

"Only one other," he replied. "Ayesha will be his favored wife, I think. In theory, they must all be treated equally, but people are human, and find a way around laws when they are in love. I must go and meet the bridegroom."

Leitrim left, and Melora turned to Trimmer. "He didn't try very hard to find a way to get Ayesha for himself. I wonder if he really loves her at all."

"I daresay the problem is that she didn't love him enough to disobey her brother."

"You mean he actually asked her!"

"I mean nothing of the sort. He couldn't get near her at all. He said she always darted off, any time he spotted her in the castle and tried to approach her. Poor Leitrim, he is feeling blue today," she said, and looked sharply to see how this was received. "You must be a little kind to him, Melora."

It was impossible to be kind to a gentleman who paid so little heed to her. Leitrim fell into conversation with Murad's son and Rashid. When his mind and eyes strayed from business, it was toward the bride that they wandered. Leitrim stole discreet glances at the pale face behind the veil, and felt not a sense of loss, but a sense of frustration that he had never known that woman he thought he might have come to love.

Melora had no chance to be kind till the party was over, and the bride had left for her new home. By the time she was back in her own apartment, she was in no mood for kindness.

"When I marry," she said, "I shall have a grand do, with feasting and dancing till dawn. And I shan't sit on the sidelines like Ayesha, just watching the men dance either. I shall dance every waltz."

"I'm relieved to hear it," Leitrim said. "That means you've given up any idea of marrying Rashid. If you married him, you would behave as Ayesha behaved today. Don't think Rashid would stand still for his wife making a display of herself."

She gave him a condescending glance. "The great expert on Shaikh Rashid speaks again, misinforming the world on a subject of which he is nearly totally ignorant. I know Rashid better than you do by now. I know how to handle him,'' she boasted.

"You won't 'handle' a husband as easily as you handle a temporarily infatuated bachelor,'' he warned her. "Once the bird is lured into the nest, the hawk will show its claws.''

"The prey has claws of its own.''

"A pity it has only a bird brain.''

"Children, children!'' Miss Trimmer shouted. "Have pity on an old lady's head. My ears ache from that dreadful squeaky music we had to listen to for hours. Let us have a nice cup of tea, and some peace and quiet.''

"I'm sorry, Trimmer,'' Leitrim said, and rose to leave. "I'll ask the servants to send hot water.''

When he was gone, Trimmer turned a sapient eye on her charge. "Is that your notion of kindness, to rip up at the poor lad? Anyone can see he is grieving.''

"I saw nothing of the sort.''

"You can't judge a book by its pages, Melora. You should know that by now.''

"I'm sick and tired of his telling me what Rashid is like. He doesn't know Rashid as I do. I'll show him.''

"I'm almost afraid to ask—how do you plan to do that?''

"This party Rashid is holding for us . . . I shall show Lord Leitrim that Rashid can be made to behave like a proper English gentleman.''

"I wish he would serve some proper English food. Do you realize, Melora, we haven't had any vegetables since we've been here?''

"They don't grow many vegetables in this part

of the world. The fruit is delicious though.''

"Yes, my dear, but wouldn't you give your eye tooth for a nice potato, and some peas and asparagus. Even cabbage, though I detest it.''

"I don't miss them at all. And I particularly despise potatoes. They always remind me of Ireland.''

On this angry speech, Melora went out to the balcony and stared at the familiar view. A wedding should be a happy event, but Ayesha's wedding had made her ineffably sad. She didn't want to be alone, and soon returned inside.

"Weddings are important, aren't they, Trimmer?'' she said vaguely. "I mean births and weddings and deaths—those are the main events of life. That didn't seem like a wedding to me. I wouldn't feel married if . . . oh, I don't know.''

"What you missed was the old traditional ritual of an English wedding. Life is nothing without its rituals, to dress it up. They are what gives meaning to this strange life of ours. Paying morning calls and making debuts and being presented at Court. Give up that, and what are we? A bunch of animals, mating and breeding and eeking out an existence. You can't give up the rituals of a lifetime, Melora, and you can't switch horses in midstream. You are an English lady, and you're not going to become an Arab by hanging a veil over your face and hiding your white skin.''

"But what of love?''

"My foolish girl, love is not a ritual!''

"Then what is it?''

"It is God's little joke on us. When we begin to think we are rational creatures, he pitches us into love, and sits in heaven splitting his sides laughing while we untangle ourselves. I am on to Him. That is why I never married. That and Mr. Herbert's not asking me, of course.'' She was interrupted by a knock at the door. ''Ah, here is our hot water! So kind of Leitrim. He understands what is important to us. He would never leave us without the means of making tea.''

Chapter Twelve

"But in my country, a distinguished visiting lady guest does not dance, Melora," the *shaikh* said firmly. "That is work for hired performers."

The visit was one of many that occurred between the honored English guests and Shaikh Rashid, in preparation for his European party. Lord Leitrim was present, as well as Miss Trimmer. Both ladies now wore their English gowns. The tea pot now wore its tea cosy. It was Shaikh Rashid who looked out of place in his own salon.

"But as it is to be a European-style party, Rashid," Melora pointed out, "should the entertainment not also be in the European manner? At home, the ladies and gentlemen dance—with each other."

"Gentlemen dancing?" Rashid exclaimed, and laughed heartily. "Next you will tell me they curl their hair, and wear petticoats."

"Not petticoats," she admitted, "though I have known more than one fop to do his hair up in papers."

"This dancing," Rashid said, "what sort of music is required?"

"Violins, piano, cello," Melora said. Her eyes slid to the piano in the corner. "Miss Trimmer plays the piano."

"You will show me how this dancing is performed," the *shaikh* decided.

"I can't do it alone," she protested. "Michael—perhaps you—"

"We'd require three more people to form a set," Leitrim pointed out.

"Not for the waltz," she replied.

"I have heard of your cotillion and minuet, but a waltz?" Rashid asked.

"It is becoming the rage at home," she assured him. "In Bombay, all the new arrivals from England were doing it. Miss Trimmer, you know the famous waltz from Gardel's *Dansomanie*. Come, Michael. Let us demonstrate the waltz for the *shaikh*."

Michael rose and gave her his hand. "Are you trying to give the man a heart attack?" he asked.

"No, trying to convince him dancing isn't immoral."

"He doesn't consider it immoral, only infra dig."

Miss Trimmer went to the pianoforte and began playing. Leitrim put his arm around Melora and they began to follow the music. Shaikh Rashid leaned forward in his eagerness to see this spectacle. The rippling rhythm sounded unusual to him. Even more unusual was to see a gentleman place his arm around a lady in public—the lady smile and place her hand on his shoulder. He sat mesmerized as the couple swirled and glided around the room. How did they do it without stepping on each other's feet? He stared at Leitrim's moving feet. Step, slide, step. That seemed easy enough. But only see how they spun and turned and glided. He could never master it. And it seemed the style to keep up a lively conversation at the same time.

"You must have been practicing, Michael," Melora said. "How did you learn to dance the new waltz so competently?"

"You never have to ask an Irishman whether he knows how to dance or drink. They come 'natural' to us, like making love."

"And talking nonsense," she added.

"I grant you the laurel in that line. Adding dancing to the party is a poor idea, Melora. The only English ladies present will be you and Trimmer, and as Trimmer has to play the piano—"

She smiled in satisfaction. "Then that leaves only me, to dance with all the gentlemen. What a pity! You must get your name on my card early, or you'll end up dancing with Captain Redding."

"I should prefer to watch the *shaikh*'s dancing girls. You're out in your reckoning if you hope to incite Rashid to passion by this poor display of lechery."

"Lechery! You sound like a Methodist!"

"I'm no Methodist. You'll notice I'm dancing on both legs. They only use one."

She glanced toward the sofa and noticed how closely the *shaikh* was observing them. "We've incited him to interest at least. I think he's trying to see how the waltz is done. I'm going to make him dance with me."

"And I'm going to convert him to Christianity," Leitrim replied ironically.

She gave him a saucy smile. "You think I can't do it?"

"I know you can't."

When the piece was ended, Melora went to Rashid and offered him her hand. "Your turn, Your Excellency," she said.

She saw the indecision on his face, and saw as well that he was longing to give it a try. It was only his dignity that deterred him. "I'll show you the steps," she said. "It's really very simple." Rashid rose and allowed himself to be drawn into it.

"You count one, two, three," she explained. "The gentleman steps backward with the left foot, then the right, then the left again. That's all. Then you repeat it, in time to the music. Trimmer, play the waltz again, please."

Rashid performed the steps, slowly, uncertainly at first. But his natural sense of rhythm soon took over, and before long he was waltzing. Melora realized it was her role to assume responsibility for any missteps. "Sorry," she smiled, when he trod on her toes.

After three 'sorry's', Rashid said, "It is my robes that cause the problem."

"If you wore trousers it would be easier."

Rashid gave her a sharp look. "*You* are not wearing trousers, however. The robe is not at fault. It is I who am slow to learn these dancing tricks, and blame it on my innocent robes."

"Perhaps you're right. I would love to see you in an English-style evening suit," she said leadingly.

"The party is in three days. There is not time to send to England, and my seamstresses do not fabricate trousers."

"Pity," she sighed.

Rashid looked at Leitrim, who had moved to stand at the piano beside Trimmer. In his uniform, he looked very gallant. The jacket displayed his broad shoulders and narrow waist to great advantage. Rashid too had broad shoulders and a stomach flat as a table. Why should he hide his excellent physique under a blanket? Duval knew a French tailor in the village. Perhaps—

Then his mind wandered to other things. It felt uncommonly strange to hold in his arms a beautiful, pale lady, with her chaperone and another man in the same room. What an extraordinary woman she was! She had ridden for hours in the hot desert sun, and never complained. She argued with gentlemen, and often won her point. Now she was chattering like a magpie, and still her dainty feet moved with the music, evading his clumsy toes at every move. It was like flying, this insane waltz. As good as the rest was to see Leitrim's jealous eyes follow them. He began to whirl and swirl, gliding over the floor like a bird in flight. It was madness, and he adored it. But he would not subject himself to performing these tricks in front of company at his party.

When the meeting was over, Leitrim accompanied the ladies upstairs. Melora was crowing with her success at making Rashid dance. "And you said I couldn't tame him!" she boasted to Leitrim.

"One swallow doesn't make a spring."

"But it tells of the end of winter, sir. Come now, confess you're amazed at my success."

"I am stunned, but I hope that before spring arrives, you'll be out of here. Redding's ship is about ready to sail. In fact, it will leave in three days. For God's sake don't mention it to Duval at the party. We don't want him preparing any little surprises for us."

"That soon!"

He stared at her, and noticed no joy. "That soon," he said curtly, and rushed forward to hold the door for Miss Trimmer.

Flowers filled the European salon. Shaikh Rashid paced back and forth, adjusting a cushion here, rearranging a vase on the table. He glanced up and caught his reflection in the *ormolu* mirror over the sofa. How handsome he looked in this European suit after all. The ruffled white of his shirt front against the black jacket reminded him of the Christian nuns, whom he had seen in his travels. Of course the sisters did not wear a large *cabochon* ruby at their throat. Was it too gaudy? Duval always wore a diamond in his cravat. He straightened his shoulders, pulled in his stomach and stretched his neck. The cravat felt like a noose around it.

In the mirror, he caught a moving reflection and turned guiltily around, for he didn't wish his servants to see him admiring himself. It was not the servants, but his house guests, come to join the party. He went into the hallway to greet them. How lovely she looked, though he was a little disappointed Melora wasn't wearing blue. The pale

green of her gown reminded him of sea foam. She
was Venus, rising from the waves—with that
omnipresent Adonis clutching at her elbow. Damn
the man!

"Rashid!" Melora exclaimed, and rushed
forward, her smile a blaze of sunshine. "You did
it! Oh Trimmer! Doesn't he look handsome!"

"A surprise for you," Rashid said, and bowed.
"I took your advice and came *à l'anglaise.*"

"But how did you manage it?"

"Monsieur Duval was kind enough to send his
tailor to me. I am in the proper mode, Lord
Leitrim?" he asked.

Leitrim examined him stiffly. The gentlemen
assessed each other like bantam cocks, preparing to
fight. "Weston couldn't do better," he allowed.
"Weston is our premier tailor in London, Your
Excellency."

Shaikh Rashid examined the ribbons and
medals, that added a bright splash of color to the
competition's uniform, and was glad he had worn
the ruby. "I find the trousers very comfortable,"
he said. "The cravat, however—"

"You'll get used to it," Melora said, and putting
her hand on his elbow, she walked into the room
with him. She looked all around and exclaimed, "I
could just imagine I am at home. Everything is
superb, Rashid."

"The dining, I fear, will be on low tables. There
was not time to arrange an English decor, but I
am serving mutton. That is the preferred English
dish, I think?"

"Lovely." Her smile was a glow of pleasure, for
she knew all this trouble and expense were for her
sole benefit.

There was a knocking at the door, and soon the guests began arriving. Captain Redding and his half-dozen officers were first, followed by Monsieur Duval. Sherry was served, and the company settled in for some pre-dinner conversation.

Captain Redding and his officers sat conversing with the *shaikh*. Duval turned his chair toward the ladies' corner and spoke quietly to Miss Trimmer.

"A lovely party. Is it to be a farewell do for you, ladies? I expect you will be leaving soon. I know the Reliant is repaired."

Leitrim, who sat halfway between the two groups, turned an alarmed face toward Trimmer and Duval. "When it leaves, the Bombay Buccaneers will be out in force to accompany it. I just mention the fact in case you happen to be speaking to any pirates," he said sardonically. "How is the translation of the Koran going, monsieur?" he asked swiftly, to kill the subject. "Have you managed to find a Muslim scholar to help you?"

"Yes, I am very busily at work on it," Duval told him, but he was not deceived by the reason for the question. He must pursue his conversation with the English ladies later.

"I went to see a mosque," Melora told him. "I think it very shabby of the gentlemen not to allow us to go inside. I should love to see it."

Leitrim hastily took up this subject, to avoid the more dangerous one. "There isn't much to see, actually. It's mostly an empty space."

"But still," Melora persisted, "when one travels to foreign lands, she wants to see the points of interest. Museums and churches and palaces— those are the sorts of things everyone at home will want to know about.''

"No Muslim would permit you to enter his mosque, but surely Shaikh Rashid could arrange for you to have a peek in,'' Duval said. He gave a meaningful smile and added, "You have considerable influence in that quarter, I think? His Excellency speaks very highly of you.''

"No, I've already asked him.''

Duval gave her hand a consoling pat. "If the honor were mine to bestow, you would be taken to view a service, milady. Unfortunately a poor scholar such as I has little influence.''

"How kind of you, monsieur,'' Melora smiled.

A servant appeared and announced in what was obviously phonetic English, "Deener iss serve.''

Leitrim moved to Melora's side and whispered, "Duval is fishing for information. Don't tell him when Redding's ship is leaving.''

She smiled to prevent Duval's suspicion and said, "I know. Best remind Trimmer.''

"I shall, at once.'' He glided off to do it immediately.

The *shaikh* gave Leitrim a sharp look and placed a proprietary hand on Melora's arm. Together, they led the party into the dining room. "It is the custom for the guest of honor to sit on the host's right hand, no?'' he asked, showing her to a seat beside him. "Though our table lacks chairs, I am employing the English system in your honor. Miss Trimmer is acting as my hostess at the end of the table.''

Miss Trimmer was lowered to the floor by Leitrim and one of the junior officers. She found that with a pile of pillows at her back, and stretching her legs out under the table, she was not entirely uncomfortable.

The table, though lacking chairs, was set in some semblance of the European manner, with cutlery and china. Rashid looked hopefully to his companion for a compliment. "Very nice, Rashid," she said. "All that is lacking is more ladies. At home, we usually seat ladies and gentlemen alternatively at the table, to enliven the conversation."

"An English preacher from India once told me the essence of good manners was to put everyone at ease. I did not want to inflame the officers to jealousy, so I kept you for myself, with Duval having the honor on the other side."

Duval, listening, smiled. "I have got the best of this arrangement," he said, with a bow to Melora.

Melora saw from the corner of her eye that Rashid handled his cutlery like a proper gentleman. There was no soup served, but a variety of fish dishes filled the lack. The mutton had been roasted on a spit and carved before being brought to the table. Surrounded by the vivacious young officers, Melora soon forgot she was not at home, and enjoyed the party. Wine was plentiful, and everyone drank.

Duval inclined his head toward Melora and said in a low voice, "His Excellency has put himself to much trouble with this affair. You, I think, are the cause of it?"

"I teased him into it," she admitted.

Across the table, Leitrim came to attention and tried to overhear their conversation.

Duval listened and assumed an avuncular pose.

"There would be many difficulties arranging a match between the two of you," he pointed out. "Oil and water don't mix."

She lifted her chin pugnaciously. "Which of us are you calling water, monsieur? Me? I'm not sure I like being compared to such a bland beverage."

He laughed. "Oil and champagne is more like it. The maxim still holds true. You are aware that Muslims are permitted four wives?"

Rashid turned jealously and said, "You are instructing Lady Melora in Islamic ways, Duval? That would best be left to an expert."

"I was just mentioning the inherent difficulties, Your Excellency. A Muslim cannot marry a Christian."

"You are mistaken, monsieur," the *shaikh* said firmly. "A Muslim lady may not marry anyone but a Muslim. A Muslim man may marry a Muslim or a *Kitabiya*—one who believes in a religion revealed to her by a book—such as the Bible. He may not marry an atheist, for example."

"And the four wives?" Duval persisted.

"This is allowed," Rashid said. "It is not obligatory, however. A man may possess a pistol and not fire it."

"Still," Duval persisted, "I should think a lady would feel a trifle uncomfortable with a loaded pistol in her husband's hand."

"It was a poor metaphor," Rashid admitted. "I should have said a man may possess wealth and choose not to spend it. No lady would object to having a wealthy husband."

Melora looked across the table at Leitrim. His annoyance with the conversation was obvious on his glowering visage. She lifted her glass and sipped, with a flame of mischief dancing in her eyes.

"While Mohammed's wife, Khadijah, lived," Rashid continued, "he took no other wives." He turned a steady gaze to Melora. "I am a great admirer of Mohammed," he said.

"But all in all," Duval continued "Mohammed had several marriages."

"This is true," Rashid nodded. "Marriages are often used here, as in your western countries, to form political alliances. Take care, Duval, or you will accomplish what you wish to avoid. England, you know, wishes for an alliance with me at this time."

Melora bristled up. Regarding her across the table, Leitrim smiled and said, "How romantic! At home, only queens and princesses are required to make such sensible matches, Your Excellency. Most young ladies nowadays marry for love."

Rashid listened. "When love and expediency coexist," he pointed out, "we have what Voltaire calls 'the best of all possible worlds.' "

"Quite," Leitrim agreed. "And we know how good Cunegonde's and Candide's world was."

Duval laughed aloud. "Lord Leitrim has gained a point on you there, Your Excellency. As a Frenchman, milord, I am flattered that you turn to French literature to clinch your argument. One *does* become tired of forever hearing Shakespeare dragged out as the last word."

Rashid lifted a quizzing brow. "I would not assume we have heard the last word on this matter yet, monsieur, but we shall speak of other things now.''

Servants began removing dishes and food, and others came with huge platters of fruit and trays of sweets. Rashid selected a fig for Melora with great care, peeled it and set it on her plate. When Rashid turned to speak to Captain Redding on his other side, Duval leaned closer to Melora.

"Are you seriously entertaining the notion of marrying the *shaikh*?" he asked.

"A lady never entertains such an idea till she has been asked, monsieur. The *shaikh* has not asked me to marry him."

"It would be a deuced lonesome life for a young lady, cut off from her family and friends. You have no idea how restricted it would be, once the first glow of romance faded. Stuck off in a *seraglio* with his other wives and all their children—I would think more than twice about such a fate, Lady Melora. You are not under his hand at the moment, so he allows you the latitude of an honored guest. Once he had you in his power, things would change. He would not allow you to meet with your friend Leitrim, for example. A Muslim keeps his wives to himself."

"Rashid would not necessarily marry any other wives."

"The rumor in the village is that he plans to marry Shaikh Amir bin Hamad's daughter to settle an alliance between their two houses. For many years it has been understood he would marry her."

"That's not true!" she exclaimed at once. "He would have told me if it were so." What did Duval know about anything?

"If you say so, madame," Duval said. He gave her a disbelieving look, then turned to his food.

Melora became pensive as she pondered Duval's warning. It was one often heard from Leitrim and Trimmer. It was interesting to visit the *shaikh* as a guest, but could she endure the privations of a *shaikh's* wife? Would he treat her as an Englishwoman, or as a possession?

When dinner was over, the ladies retired to the European salon while the gentlemen took their port. "You notice Duval was fishing for information?" Melora mentioned.

"I learned something interesting from Redding," Trimmer replied. "Leitrim hasn't been quite frank with us. It is tomorrow we leave. Leitrim didn't trust us to keep the secret from Duval. I am quite angry with young Leitrim. Doesn't he realize we have all our packing to attend to?"

"Tomorrow? And he wasn't going to tell us!"

"Aye, he takes matters very much into his own hands."

"He wants to spirit me away before Rashid has a chance to speak—"

Trimmer bit her lip. If that was Leitrim's thinking, she was sorry she had revealed the truth. "Perhaps Rashid knows," she said, and received a strong argument against that possibility.

When Melora glanced up, Shaikh Rashid stood at the doorway, gazing at her. Behind him the officers and Duval formed a group, adding a note of familiarity. All the warnings fell from her like magic, and a soft smile curved her lips as the two gazed silently at each other. Then the *shaikh* stepped into the room, heading straight for her.

"Is it time for the dance now?" Melora asked.

"Unfortunately, no. It has been decided there

will be no dancing,'' he said.

"But you are the one who makes decisions, Rashid!"

"I have decided against it,'' he said simply. "It would be cruel for me to monopolize the only young lady in the room, and it would be too cruel for you to dance with anyone else. This is not the time for waltzing. We shall do that another time.''

"You know I shall be leaving soon,'' she reminded him, and looked with interest for his reply. "Very soon. Sooner, perhaps, than you think.''

"If you stayed forever, Melora, it would not be long enough.''

"But I am *not* staying forever.''

"You cannot leave me. 'God obligeth no man to more than he hath given him ability to endure','' he said, and smiled enigmatically. "That is a quotation from the Koran, Melora. No doubt your Bible says something similar. The two great books are not inimical.''

"I can't stay,'' she said, and looked at him sadly. "You know I couldn't live the way your women live in this country.''

"Someone has been giving you an improper idea of how women are treated here. We respect our women, as the Koran urges. 'Oh men, respect women who have borne you.' This occurs in Chapter Four. I have been studying the book a good deal lately, seeking guidance in this dilemma. It is Allah who holds our destiny in his hands. I find nothing in my reading that prohibits a marriage between us. It infringes on my duties to neither Allah, nor to my people. I shall discuss this further with my *kalifah*. Now I must speak to my other guests." He bowed and left.

Leitrim joined Melora as soon as Shaikh Rashid was gone. She turned a fiery eye on him. "Well, Leitrim! It seems you neglected to tell me something." He looked at her questioningly.

"Never mind putting on that innocent Irish face. Redding let it slip to Trimmer that we're leaving tomorrow. How dare you arrange this without telling me?"

"I meant to tell you tonight."

"At what hour is the ship leaving?"

"Tomorrow afternoon at three. And not a minute too soon, to judge by the cow eyes you and Rashid have been exchanging."

"Does he know?"

"No, he doesn't."

Melora's fingers clutched at her skirts. Tomorrow! Her eyes sought out Rashid, as he stood talking with Captain Redding. He had never looked more attractive. Tall, dark, suave. The evening suit took the edge of strangeness from him. He seemed at home, amongst her people.

"Clothes don't really make the man, you know," Leitrim warned her. "You have had more success than I thought possible, but beneath that black jacket beats the heart of a *shaikh*, with all that that implies."

"I find him charming," she said simply.

"I wish I could get you out of here tonight."

Duval strolled over and joined them. "What do you think of this romance between Lady Melora and the *shaikh*?" he asked.

"Romance?" Leitrim asked, as though

confused. "Lady Melora was just urging me to set a fire under Captain Redding. She is most eager to get home. Enjoy the few days you have left, my dear," he said, then bowed and went to his fellow officers.

Duval waggled a finger at her playfully. "You are a naughty girl, Lady Melora, fooling the nice Captain."

"Nice?" she snipped. "He's horrid."

"We say at home the English milords are carved from ice. I have given thought to what you said earlier about the mosque. It is a pity for you to go home without seeing it. Shaikh Rashid would not take you inside, but perhaps I might arrange it, if you wish."

She looked interested. "Could you?" she asked.

"It would have to be done with the greatest secrecy. The *shaikh* would be angry with me—and you!—if he learned."

"Perhaps we could arrange it tomorrow morning."

"Morning?" he asked doubtfully. "No, the thing must be done under cover of darkness. Tomorrow evening, perhaps, when everyone has retired."

But by tomorrow evening she might be miles out at sea. "Couldn't we go tonight?"

Duval smiled in approval. "You are what the bucks call the game chick, Lady Melora. Tonight it is! I shall have a horse waiting outside the castle walls two hours after I leave."

"Must it be so late?"

"There are arrangements to be made. I must bring you a mount. And you must dress up in a *burnous*. Make yourself look like a man, if such a thing is possible. And when you return to England, you will be the only lady ever to have a firsthand description of a mosque. Your Miss Trimmer—she will agree?"

"Good gracious no. I must slip out after she is asleep. Perhaps two hours is not too soon. But we must be home before dawn."

"We shall go to the closest one, behind the *souk*. It is only an hour away. With me, you will be perfectly safe. You should leave by the back door of the castle. Shaikh Rashid leaves guards out front. There is a gate in the walls beside the stable. You know the way?" She nodded.

Monsieur Duval smiled and strolled on to chat to some of the officers. He smiled contentedly at his success. He would leave now. The sooner this do broke up, the sooner he could get on with it. The way things were progressing, he feared the chit might actually pull off her weddng to Rashid. That would be disastrous for him. Rashid would sign the truce and start calling himself Mister—or milord. This would take care of Lady Melora.

After Duval left, Captain Redding and his crew took their leave too.

"A marvelous party, Your Excellency," Miss Trimmer complimented Rashid.

"Lovely," Melora added.

"Before you leave, Miss Trimmer," Rashid said, "would you play a waltz for us? I think Melora is not completely satisfied with her party till she has danced."

Leitrim looked as though he wanted to object. A hot anger welled up inside when Melora smiled at the *shaikh* and gave him her hand. "The one from *Dansomanie*, Trimmer," she said.

Trimmer went to the piano and in the salon, nearly empty now, Melora and Rashid danced to the intoxicating strains of the waltz.

Chapter Thirteen

"What did Duval have to say?" Leitrim asked,
when he accompanied the ladies to their bedroom
after the party. The *shaikh,* he was happy to see,
went to visit with his religious advisor.

"Nothing of any interest," Melora answered
blandly.

Studying her, Leitrim noticed she was not
completely at ease. "You didn't let slip that we're
leaving tomorrow?" he asked.

"Of course not."

"The man's a viper. He'll make mischief if he
can. Oh well," he said, "he can't do much harm in
one more day."

Melora listened, and felt a shiver of appre-
hension at her plans for meeting Duval. If he was
as treacherous as Michael thought, she shouldn't
go.

Miss Trimmer stifled a yawn and said, "I'm for

bed. Don't stay late, Leitrim. We must be up early tomorrow to oversee our packing.''

"I'll be leaving presently,'' he assured her. But when he was alone with Melora, he seemed disinclined to part from her. "What was Rashid saying, as you waltzed with him?'' he asked. The glint of interest in his eyes belied the casual tone.

She walked toward the open doors of the balcony and went out into the moonlight, with Leitrim following. They looked together at the black velvet sky, spangled with stars and a moon reflecting in the ocean beyond.

"He didn't say much. He has to count while he waltzes.''

"His expression didn't look like 'one, two, three' to me—nor yours either.''

He expected a pert answer. Melora just looked at him a moment, rather sadly. "What shall I do, Michael?'' she asked.

"Do? About what?''

"About Rashid. I—I think he loves me. And I know I love him. I've never met anyone so . . . Oh, you know.''

"Keep your two feet on the ground, and set your course straight toward England. Any notion that you could be comfortable here is an illusion, Melora. As insubstantial as a desert mirage.''

Melora smiled in memory. "Rashid says you see what your heart most desires in a mirage. That's why most people see water in the desert. I saw water—and I saw Rashid and myself standing at its edge.''

A worried frown pinched his brow. He reached and covered Melora's hand with his. "In India, I met a woman.''

She looked up with interest. When she spoke, there was a note of pique in her voice. "Oh! You never mentioned her before."

"Somehow we always end talking about *your* problems."

"Was she pretty?"

"Sara was beautiful, a gentle, loving girl. She was an Anglo-Indian—her father was an English Captain. He died when she was young, however, and she was raised by her mother. She wore our sort of clothing, spoke English flawlessly, had a proper nanny when she was young and all that. She had clear gray eyes and hair as black as jet, long and soft and silky. I wanted to marry her."

"I hope you pursued her more vigorously than you did Ayesha."

"She was more pursuable. We discussed marriage. We had nearly come to terms. I was describing my home to her—we raise beef cattle at Drumcliff. 'But how do you make any money?' she asked, and I realized in that one question the world of difference between us. I make money by selling what, to her, was sacred. Her father had her baptized a Christian—she even went to church on Sundays, but she had assimilated the customs and beliefs of the culture that nourished her. No one can escape the past, Melora. Not my Sara, not Rashid, not you."

"Rashid realizes I'm different from Moslem women."

"In his mind he realizes it, but in his heart, you're more a woman than an English woman." He peered down at her wistful face and continued trying to discourage her. "Women don't count for much here. According to Muslim belief, of the thousand merits bestowed on mankind, woman received only one; men the other nine hundred and ninety-nine. Women here are considered as children—pretty, troublesome, entertaining, but not quite—how shall I say it—rational. Never in charge of their own destiny.''

''But he loves me! I'm sure he does.''

''He loves you, but not as an equal. And the more he loves you, the more he'll want to keep you to himself. You'll be swaddled in veils from head to toe, living, no doubt, in the finest harem in all of Persia, and wearing a king's ransom in jewelry. But will you be happy?''

She considered it a moment, and drew a deep sigh. ''Not with him—like that—and not without him. It was the marriage ceremony that set me to thinking.''

''Love's a strange thing, isn't it?'' he asked gently. ''I thought my heart would crumble when I had to give up Sara. Life loomed before me as an ordeal, yet now—'' He hunched his shoulders. ''I've come to realize she was my fantasy woman. We all try to turn our first love into a fantasy. Wait till your second love comes along, and makes Rashid a pleasant memory.'' Melora looked dissatisfied with his advice.

''Has he actually asked you to marry him?''

''No, but he doesn't know we're leaving tomorrow. I want you to tell him, Michael.''

''If I'd told him tonight, Duval might have found it out. I'll tell him shortly before you leave.''

''If he asks, perhaps I shan't be leaving at all.''

''Never to see home again?'' he asked, and observed her reaction. She frowned unhappily, and Leitrim took her other hand in his. ''It's nine-

tenths sexual attraction, you know," he told her.
"Rashid's a handsome rascal, but once you're over
your affair with his marvelous dark eyes, you'll
find he's just a man, like Redding—or me."

Melora gripped her lower lip between her teeth.
"Oh, why does love have to be so difficult!" she
exclaimed. "It should be simple."

"Simple as a kiss," he agreed, and used it as an
excuse to place a light kiss on her cheek. He closed
his eyes, and let his lips linger a moment. Her face
was warm. At this close range, he smelled the
tantalizing fragrance of jasmine where the breeze
stirred her hair. Overcome by a surge of desire, he
pulled her into his arms and crushed her against
him protectively.

"Don't do it, Melora," he said, in a husky voice.

She stepped back in surprise and stared at him.
"Michael!"

"Sorry," he said, and pulled away. "I got
carried away. Blame it on the moonlight."

Her first flash of surprise changed to confusion.
For a moment, she had wanted him to kiss her.
Moonlight madness—but she felt dissatisfied, and
ill at ease with him now.

"I must go. Trimmer will be waiting," she said
primly, but she looked with interest to see if he
objected.

"Let her wait."

Leitrim pulled her back in his arms. For a
moment he just looked at her, with the moonlight
mirrored in her eyes. Then he kissed her soundly.
Melora closed her eyes and gave herself up to the
sensations of the moment. Her senses, roused to
excitement by the past weeks of attraction to
Rashid, were ready for this assault. A flame

quivered and leapt to life inside her. Her veins felt as though quicksilver was coursing through them, and her hand rose of its own volition to touch his neck. The bristle of masculine hair excited her. The pressure of his lips moving restively on hers intoxicated her. She felt Leitrim's fingers on her naked shoulder, squeezing it.

Then, as suddenly as he had pulled her into his arms, he released her. "Why did you do that?" she asked, staring at him.

"Why didn't you stop me?"

"I didn't want to. Michael—"

His fingers clutched hers till her hands felt numb. "Remember what I told you," he said. "Marriage is too important to be rushed into pell-mell."

Then he was gone, and she stood on alone in the moonlight, thinking confused thoughts. "Damn, I wish he hadn't done that," she murmured.

She went back into the room and sat with her chin in her cupped hand, thinking. Miss Trimmer was already in bed in the adjoining room. Wine always made her drowsy, and she had had a good deal of wine that night. As soon as Melora heard the deep, even breaths of her chaperone, she took up her wrap and crept relucantly, silently out of the room, down the long, dark corridor toward the staircase. High on the walls, torches burned at regular intervals to throw a dim light below. The stone staircase gave no revealing squawk as she hurried down. She wouldn't go with Duval, but she really ought to tell him, and not leave the poor man waiting.

Near the front door, a servant slept, squatting on the floor with a sword beside him. She turned the corner to the side door, unbolted it as quietly as she could, and went out into the shadowed night.

The stable yard by moonlight looked romantic. The irregular surface of the cobblestones was rough underfoot, but its irregularities were visible. She had no trouble finding the gate. She looked all around, then slipped out beyond the walls.

In a moment, a dark form detached itself from the wall and came toward her.

"Lady Melora, you are punctual," Duval said softly. "But you're wearing your evening gown."

"I've come to tell you I can't go with you, monsieur. I'm terribly sorry for having put you to so much trouble."

"What has happened to change your mind?" he asked in confusion.

"I just don't think it's a good idea. If anyone should find out—"

"You didn't tell anyone, I hope?" he exclaimed swiftly. "This escapade could ruin my reputation."

"No, of course I didn't."

He breathed a sigh of relief. "Ah, good. You're sure I can't convince you? You would have an intriguing story to tell your friends when you return home."

"I have many stories to amuse my friends. I must go now."

Duval gave a kindly smile. "I shall give you another tale to tell, milady," he said, and with a quick flash of his hand, he covered her mouth. Her eyes flew open in shock.

A small, cloaked figure leapt from the shadows. Melora tried to scream, and a gag was stuck in her mouth. She clawed at Duval, trying to get away, but he grabbed her arms and wrenched them behind her. The man drew out a rough cloth bag and threw it over her head while Duval held her arms. In the brief instant while sight remained, Melora recognized the European boy who had been taken prisoner on Redding's boat, and escaped.

For a second, Melora was too shocked to be frightened, but when her vision was cut off, she felt the onset of sheer panic. Her arms were roughly tied behind her back. She felt herself being lifted from the ground, thrown over the back of a horse—all done in complete, utter silence, that was more menacing than threats. Beneath the bag, she felt the warm, steamy flank of a horse against her cheek, smelled its pungent, horsey smell. The blood rushed to her head, that dangled uncomfortably down, with her feet hanging over the horse's other side.

She heard the jingle of harnesses and the shuffle of horses' hooves as the men mounted. One of them sat behind her on the horse, holding on to her cloak to prevent her slipping off. They spoke then, in French. The voice came from the other rider, not Duval's voice, but the younger man's. Apparently she was riding with Duval.

"I thought she was supposed to come willingly."

"A change of mind, Alphonse. It is a lady's privilege," Duval laughed.

"Are you sure she didn't tell anybody?"

"She says not. There'd be someone after us by now if she had. We'll take the detour around the first village, Alphonse, directly to the mountains."

Melora listened, trying to overcome fear and panic, to learn what she could. She had heard

Michael mention the mountains, and a fort. Something to do with the Barbary Coast pirates. Oh God, and hadn't he said it was impregnable? Why was Duval taking her there? No one would know where she was. She should have told Michael.

The horses were urged on to a gallop. She felt the gliding movement of firm equine muscles through the bag as her head slapped against the steamy flank. She was helpless, bound and gagged, treated degradingly, as though she were a sack of grain or a slain deer. She couldn't call out, she daren't even try to throw herself off the horse's back. She might be kicked to death by the flying hooves. The sound of hoofbeats changed when the horses left the road to skirt the village, but it was impossible to discover any details. There were no sights, no telltale smells, just the stuffy, rough cloth, with the faint stench of horse coming through it.

At least she could listen, and try to learn why she had been kidnapped. Money seemed the most obvious thing, but the word didn't crop up in the isolated fragments of conversation the men exchanged.

"What will Shaikh Rashid do when he finds her gone?" the younger man asked.

"Throw a tantrum, perhaps. He has no reason to suspect me. Leitrim's his competition. Maybe he'll kill him," he said, and laughed.

Silence fell again, broken only by the soft, rapid clop-clop of the hooves over the sand. It was impossible to gauge time or distance. It seemed forever that they pelted along. The terrain changed in texture from time to time. There was a return to the harder road. After some miles, they left it again, but they weren't on soft sand. The horses made a louder sound, and picked their way more carefully along. The path seemed to incline upward. Now they were going single file. The faint bleating of sheep roused from their rest hung on the air. Were they in the mountains? The breeze felt chilly. Was it a sea breeze? Impossible to tell anything.

When at last the horses stopped, Melora felt as though every bone in her body had been shaken loose from its moorings. Duval hauled her down from the horse's back, but she was unable to stand. The blood rushed from her head, leaving her giddy.

"This way," Duval said, and pushed her in front of him along a rough path.

Monsieur Duval looked over his shoulder into the darkness beyond. There was no movement, and no sound. The little fool had gone to meet him without telling a soul. A smile of satisfaction beamed. Before him lay the fortress at Raz-al-Khaimah. It was a sprawling gray hulk, nestled in a fertile valley in the mountains, protected by the hills and mountains behind, and the countless inlets of the sea coast in front. Once inside its walls, the girl was hidden as safely as though she were at the bottom of the sea.

Lady Melora's foot caught a stone and she stumbled. Duval took her by the shoulder and dragged her along toward a low door, guarded by a man in a *burnous,* armed with a sword. Melora knew by the sudden absence of breeze and the flat surface underfoot that she was in a building, and assumed they had reached the fort. She was pushed along a narrow, dark hallway, around winding corridors. She heard a heavy key turn in a lock, the

clanking of a door being opened, and she was
shoved into a cell.

The bag was pulled unceremoniously from her
head and she looked around, trying to get her
bearings. The place looked like a prison. There
were stone walls, a thick slab of roughhewn
wooden door, a rush light stuck in a wall bracket.
High on one wall was a narrow slit of window with
no glass. A three-legged stool and a chair were the
only furnishings.

Duval gave a sneering laugh and went to the
door to call for wine. A native servant brought the
bottle—no glass. Duval, who had always seemed so
civilized, pulled the cork out with his teeth and
drank deeply. Over the bottle, his eyes stared at her
till she felt her flesh creep.

He raised the bottle. *"A votre très benne santé,
mam'selle,"* he said, making a parody of a bow,
and he drank again, wiping his mouth on his coat
sleeve. When he had finished, he laughed
menacingly.

Though her insides were quaking, Melora lifted
her chin and said bravely, "Shaikh Rashid-al-
Qasimi knows I was meeting you. He'll have you
drawn, quartered and fed to the vultures for this."

"He wouldn't go to so much trouble for a
woman. This affair will quench his ardor for the
little *anglaise*, and kill any talk of a troublesome
marriage. When my men are through with you,
you'll be lucky if he'll have you for a mistress. And
don't think he won't be grateful to me in the end.
All he wants is your body, my fine lady. No need to
put himself to the trouble of a mixed marriage for
that, and offending Shaikh Amir bin Hamad into

the bargain, eh?'' He gave her a derisive look.
"Rashid doesn't know you were meeting me. He
wouldn't have permitted it. No more would
Leitrim. No, mam'selle, no one knows you're
here."

Melora swallowed painfully and tried to hide her
inner trembling. "What do you want with me?"
she asked.

"I didn't like the trend of the *shaikh's* thoughts.
His marriage of alliance with England doesn't suit
my purpose at the moment. It was only a pretext to
quiet Shaikh Amir's fury, but it might give Rashid
foolish ideas about putting an end to piracy."

She sneered. "What has the Koran to say of this,
monsieur? As a theological scholar, you've found
a precedent for kidnapping a lady, no doubt."

"You'll be no fine lady when I'm through with
you," he leered, and set the bottle aside. His bleary
eyes began a close examination of her, from head
to toe. "An appetizing bite," he grinned.

Melora read the menace in his eyes, and the
blood drained from her face. "I have money," she
said. "Let me go, and—"

"And Leitrim will come after me with a
regiment. I think not, mam'selle."

"Fifty thousand pounds!" she tempted. He
looked slightly interested. "Leitrim will come after
you in any case," she said quickly, as he seemed to
fear Leitrim more than the *shaikh*. "He suspects
you arleady. If you harm me, monsieur, he'll
hound you like a dog."

With a grunt, Duval picked up the bottle and
went toward the door, for he didn't trust himself
with the woman.

"Lock her up," he said to Alphonse.

"What if they come after her?"

"No one knows the route here. My guards are posted. You worry too much, Alphonse."

"I think we should finish her—get rid of her body in the sea. That was the plan. Then no one can prove—well, why leave evidence?"

"The 'evidence' could be worth a good deal of money. What I must do is contrive a plan to get hold of it. The old lady—Trimmer—she could prove susceptible."

Alphonse gave a 'bah' of disgust. "Greed will be the death of you, Duval."

"Just do as I say."

Alphonse looked at Lady Melora, who stared at him with dark, frightened eyes, and he drew the big brass key from his pocket.

'Get rid of her body!' The words echoed in her head. They had planned to murder her. The key turned in the lock with a deathly clank.

Chapter Fourteen

The trouble with using wine for a sleeping draught was that it made one thirsty. Miss Trimmer felt as though someone had shaken a dust cloth down her throat. She coughed discreetly into her fingers to avoid waking Melora, but the dry itch persisted. There was nothing else for it; she needed a glass of water. She sat up, pushed aside the canopy and felt around the bedside table to find the water pitcher. Her groping fingers encountered the handle, then began feeling for a glass. Really it was extremely annoying. No water glass, and the water jug weighed at least ten pounds—she couldn't sip from it. With a tsk of annoyance, she reached for the tinder box. There must be something she could use as a drinking glass.

After a few trys, she got a flame and lit the lamp, peering over her shoulder to make sure

Melora wasn't disturbed. How quietly the girl slept, not a muscle moving. Miss Trimmer glanced to the pillow, frowned, and reached across the bed to see if Melora had slid under the coverlet. Nothing. Melora was gone.

For thirty seconds she sat staring, with her mouth open. It was impossible. Becoming frightened, she lifted the lamp and glanced around the room. There was no sign of Melora's having undressed. Her slippers weren't on the floor. Her nightgown was still thrown across a chair. Trimmer tried to recall the moments before falling off to sleep. Melora had strolled out to the balcony with Leitrim. Surely she wasn't still there! She glanced at her watch. One o'clock. She'd slept for two hours.

Miss Trimmer jumped from bed and hastened into the sitting room. The balcony door was closed and bolted. Melora was nowhere to be seen. Trimmer was not of that serene disposition that meets emergencies with a cool head. Her hand holding the lamp was shaking so violently that her shadow on the wall jumped like a frightened hare. She began jabbering incoherently to herself.

"What can have happened—wretched girl. She's given me the slip. The wind tower, perhaps? Oh dear! If the *shaikh*—but perhaps she is with Leitrim—" The creases in her forehead eased somewhat, only to return with increased vigor. "Leitrim is not that sort!"

She set the lamp down, then picked it up again and paced back and forth in the room, thinking. There was no other course open; she must seek Leitrim's help. His chamber, she knew, was not far past the first corner. Trembling, she threw a peignoir over her nightgown and went down the drafty corridor in search of Leitrim, holding on to the lamp like a lifeline. A tap at his door brought no response. She knocked harder, and tried the handle. The door was locked. Was Leitrim with Melora after all? She must know. A final loud banging brought Leitrim to the door.

"Good lord, Trimmer!" he exclaimed, when he saw her. "What's the matter? Is someone ill?"

"She's gone!"

Leitrim blinked, stared, and pulled Trimmer into his room. He was in no doubt at all who 'she' was. "Do you know where?" he asked in alarm. Already he was pulling on trousers.

Trimmer noticed, amidst her confusion, that Leitrim was next door to naked. His bare chest, patched with dark hair, gave her quite a turn. She discreetly turned her head aside while he scrambled into a shirt and boots.

"I awoke a moment ago. I was thirsty—the wine, you know. She was gone. She didn't go to bed at all. Her nightgown was still on the chair. I hoped she was with you."

"I left her two hours ago."

"Where can she be?"

Leitrim gave her a sharp look. "At least we have a pretty good notion who she's with," he said grimly.

"Rashid?" Trimmer asked uncertainly.

"Who else?"

Leitrim snatched up his pistol and stuck it in the waist of his trousers. With his white shirt half open and a shock of black hair tumbling over his forehead, he strode swiftly out the door. "Go to your room, Trimmer. I'll bring her back.''

"But why—why the pistol, Leitrim?''

"It's faster than the sword,'' he replied ominously.

Trimmer trailed a few steps behind Leitrim as he hurried to Rashid's private quarters, but when she saw two guards step forward to block Leitrim's entrance, she fell back. She heard the guards' noisy protest, saw Leitrim push them aside and stride unceremoniously into Rashid's sanctum. The guards exchanged a shocked look, and each pulled a knife from the folds of his *burnous*. Trimmer felt faint with fear. She stood a moment, trying to think, then darted back to her room for her scissors, which were the closest thing to a weapon that she possessed.

Shaikh Rashid was much too troubled to sleep. To be comfortable, he had removed the evening suit and wore his own native dress. The overwhelming step he was contemplating had kept him awake for several nights. If Allah didn't wish him to marry Lady Melora, what had been his purpose in sending her here to tantalize him? He sat on pillows behind the inlaid table with his Koran open before him, seeking guidance in its wisdom. This rare work of art held the place of honor in his chamber. Its cover of hammered gold made the book heavy, and for that reason, he never removed it from the table.

He looked up in surprise when Leitrim came pelting in. Before the surprise had time to turn to anger, he saw the pistol. He was not afraid. He had faced death many times. Death was afraid of him, because he had the heart of a lion.

"You wish to speak to me, Lord Leitrim?" he asked coolly.

"Where is she?" Leitrim demanded.

The *shaikh* was quick to understand the full import of the question. The blood drained from his swarthy cheeks, and he felt now the fear that Leitrim's pistol had not brought. "She's not—" He looked over Leitrim's shoulder, where a frightened and confused Miss Trimmer had just come in, holding her scissors. "Trimmer!" Rashid exclaimed.

"She's gone, Rashid!" Miss Trimmer said simply. It was the first time she had used his name to his face.

"Shaikh Amir bin Hamad!" Rashid said. "I should have foreseen this disaster. Amir has been concerned at Lady Melora's visit. He argued violently against my contemplated marriage. So this is to be the outcome of my love for a foreigner then—a bloodbath. It is a sign from Allah."

Leitrim listened but was not convinced. "How did Amir's men get into the castle? You didn't mention any sign of violence, Trimmer?"

"I'm sure she left willingly," Trimmer agreed.

"She must have arranged to meet someone without telling us," Leitrim explained.

"One of Redding's officers, perhaps," Trimmer suggested.

Rashid turned and stared at her. "I had not thought Lady Melora to be that sort of woman!"

"She isn't," Leitrim growled. He looked ready to plough Rashid a facer.

The *shaikh* paced to and fro, his face set in rigid lines. "But who?" he demanded.

"Duval," Leitrim said grimly. "There's no one else it could be. Like a fool, I warned him against pirating the Reliant when it leaves. He's taken her to hold for ransom."

"No, to prevent my marrying her," Rashid said. "He had much to say against the marriage."

"I noticed him talking to her with a very sly smile," Leitrim worried. "He's conned her with some trumped-up story."

"We go at once," Rashid said, and went to the corner to fasten his sword around his waist. He also picked up a pistol and stowed it in a pocket of his *burnous.*

"But where does he live?" Trimmer asked.

"He has an apartment in the village," Rashid told her. "I know the place well. I have visited him there."

"He'll have taken her to his quarters at Raz-al-Khaimah," Leitrim announced. "He spends time there with Rahma b. Jabir."

Rashid stared at Leitrim. "You really think Duval is involved in Rahma's piracy? But he's not even an Arab. You never mentioned this before!"

"He was your friend—and I had no proof."

"This is worse than piracy!" We must leave at once. Raz-al-Khaimah will be difficult to penetrate," Rashid said, rubbing his chin. "The fort is well guarded. You're sure Duval has access to it?"

"He virtually runs it."

Rashid went to the door and issued terse orders to his men. "The horses will be brought out. We'll use all of them, and my best men. Perhaps one of my men will know the route to the fort. It is a closely guarded secret.''

"I know the way," Leitrim said. Rashid stared. "Best change your outfit, Shaikh. That white will make you a clear target at night."

Rashid glanced at Leitrim's white shirt. "And you, milord?" he asked. "I see the famous English sang froid has left you." He tossed Leitrim a black *burnous* and put one on himself.

Trying to think of some contribution to the effort, Miss Trimmer said, "Tea! I shall make a pot of tea to have ready for your return."

No one paid her any heed. She ran off and the men went outside to await the horses. "I don't understand how Duval convinced Melora to go with him," Rashid said.

"Then you don't understand Melora," Leitrim answered cryptically. "You have only to use the word 'can't,' and she will move heaven and bend earth to do the thing."

"This is a great flaw in a woman," Rashid said. "She must be led by her husband's wishes."

"I strongly advise you against ever visiting England, Your Excellency, or having much to do with English ladies."

When they reached the door, the courtyard was alive with the whinnying of horses and exclamations of men readying for the adventure. Rashid and Leitrim mounted the lead horses. The gate was thrown open and the cavalcade galloped into the night.

"You're sure you can find the route?" Rashid asked.

"I can find it. We'll have to leave the horses some yards from the last narrow pass. We won't all go trooping in at once to alert them. Let us avoid the bloodbath, if possible.''

"It is not a woman's place to create so much bother,'' Rashid frowned.

Leitrim gave an ironic smile. "Christian ladies are all daughters of Eve, sir. Getting Adam thrown out of paradise was just the beginning.''

They took the most direct route along the sea coast, with the moon shining indifferently on harried faces, galloping steeds, glinting off the handles of the swords, and picking out a pale flower against black foliage. Danger, death and beauty—they were all one to the night and the moonlight.

When they approached the foothills of the Marble Mountains, the pace slowed to a trot. The Arabian horses picked their way delicately over boulders and uneven terrain.

"This Sinbad is the sweetest horse I ever rode,'' Leitrim complimented. "Would you consider selling him, Your Excellency?''

"If we bring her back unharmed, Sinbad is yours, milord.''

Leitrim gave him a quick, curious look. "Unharmed—or alive?''

Rashid ignored the question. As they were now forced to proceed in single file, Leitrim had no opportunity to repeat it. He took the lead, trying to remember the route shown him by the little shepherd. He looked up at the mountain tops to take his bearings. Unfortunately, the boy had moved his flock to another patch of pasture, so wasn't there to guide them. The horses, climbing in single file up the narrow mountain pass resembled a large, black snake.

When they reached the mid point, Leitrim dismounted and after consultation with Rashid, two men were left behind to tend the mounts.

"We'll go first to reconnoiter," Leitrim suggested to Rashid. "We don't want your men alerting the guards. There'll be one at the path leading to the fort. He'll have to be put out of commission first."

Rashid drew out a short knife. "A bullet will warn the others," he said simply.

They inched their way forward, around the bends of the mountain pass. From time to time, Leitrim took his bearings by the mountain tops. He recognized the spot where the snake had found him before, and knew they were close to their destination. "Around that corner," he whispered to Rashid.

Even as he spoke, a saturnine face peered around the rock cliff—too far to reach, and too close to hope not to be seen. The guard asked a question in Arabic. "Is that you, Hajim?" Leitrim understood it, but didn't trust his accent to reply.

The *shaikh* stepped forward and gave a laughing answer. When Rashid was within touching distance of the guard, Leitrim heard a quiet grunt, and the man fell at Rashid's feet. They rolled him aside and crept furtively forward. Swaying palms gave a false impression of serenity. The fort was a massive shadow twenty yards away. It was fenced by a mud wall with cobbled walkways for animals. They advanced slowly within the wall. Leitrim pointed to a few lighted window openings in the right wing. The outline of two guards at the door was dimly visible. Rashid and Leitrim exchanged a questioning look.

"I'll call," Rashid said. "When they come, you take the one on the right. I'll take the other."

"Only one will come. The other will sound the alarm. Let me creep up closer. I'll try to stop him before he can make a racket."

Sticking to the shadows, Leitrim edged forward, closer, closer. The guards heard the furtive shuffle of booted feet and exchanged a wary look. They raised their swords. Rashid called, and one moved cautiously toward him. Leitrim didn't see the knife flash, but as there was no outcry, he assumed Rashid had succeeded. The guard remaining at the door peered into the shadows, took a step forward. Leitrim flew out at him. The man emitted one howl before he fell silent on the ground.

Leitrim tried the door. It opened with a squawk, but no one came. He and Rashid slid into the dank, stone hallway, where one torch on the wall gave very poor illumination. The fortress was huge. Half a dozen hallways opened into the distance. Remembering the lit windows, Leitrim pointed to the right corridor and proceeded quietly toward it, drawing his pistol.

Was it really going to be this easy? Duval alone, or with perhaps one other man? The door was open a crack. No voices were heard within. Leitrim edged forward, peered through the door, and saw Duval sitting at a desk, all alone, perusing what looked like a sheet of figures. He pushed the door open and entered, his pistol aimed between Duval's eyes.

"Calculating your profit, Duval?" he asked.

"You can deduct whatever you planned to make on Lady Melora."

Duval looked up and smiled innocently. "Ah, Lord Leitrim. What a delightful surprise. You have discovered my secret lair. I shan't ask what you did with my guards. Brandy?" he said, and lifted the decanter.

"Business before pleasure—I refer to the pleasure of killing you, monsieur. Where have you sequestered the lady?"

"I left Madame Duval at home in France."

"I said *lady,* monsieur," Leitrim replied sardonically.

A flame of anger leapt in Duval's eyes. "I'm afraid I don't understand, milord. There are no ladies here. Only my men—the hundred and fifty cutthroat pirates I keep for my little business enterprise. But you know all about that."

Rashid's head appeared at the door. "Leitrim! Men—dozens of them!" he called. In the distance was heard the rushing of sandaled feet and the rising murmur of voices.

Duval smiled kindly. "I alerted them when you were spotted climbing the mountain. You have entered my parlor most obligingly, gentlemen. A pity I had to sacrifice a few guards, but Allah will bring them all back at the resurrection. Is that not the message in your good book, Your Excellency?"

" 'Woe be unto those who play the hypocrite,' " Rashid said in a low, menacing voice, and he lunged for Duval's throat.

Leitrim hurried to the door and drew the heavy bolt. Quickly surveying the room, he spotted another door behind Duval's desk. "This way," he called.

Rashid hauled Duval up from the chair and pushed him through the door, as the sound of hammering at the front door began. Leitrim looked hastily around for another exit, but saw only a window. He pulled Rashid's arm and pointed to it.

Rashid glanced unconcernedly at the window, apparently impervious to the rattling of the front door in the other room. He put the fingers of his right hand around Duval's throat and held the man against the wall, as his fingers tightened. "Where is she?" he demanded fiercely. "If you've touched one golden curl on her head, I will take pleasure to cut out your heart and feed it to my dogs."

Duval's face turned red, and his voice was a gargle. "Leitrim—stop him. He's mad."

"Use your gun. It's faster," Leitrim suggested to Rashid.

Rashid's fingers dug into the soft flesh, and Duval's face deepened to purple. "Downstairs," he managed to say, before Rashid choked the life out of him.

From the next room came the unmistakable sounds of the door caving in. There was an ear-splitting crash, followed immediately by shouts and running feet. Leitrim looked at Rashid, tossed his head toward the window, and vaulted out. Rashid gave one final squeeze of his fingers before tossing Duval to the ground, gasping. Duval had just enough energy to point to the window when his men came pelting in.

A dozen of them swarmed out after Rashid and Leitrim. "Downstairs! Guard the prisoner," Duval gasped, and another batch ran back out the door, shouting in excitement.

As soon as they hit the ground, Leitrim and Rashid ran off in different directions, hoping that one of them would find Melora. Shaikh Rashid's men heard the shots as Duval's pirates opened fire, and ran toward the fort, uttering bloodcurdling cries as they advanced. Rashid urged them on, with himself at their head, gallantly brandishing a sword in one hand, his pistol in the other, as balls of fire exploded around him. No coward, the man was smiling amidst the acrid stench of gunsmoke and the explosions. When Duval made the error of sticking his head out the window, Rashid pointed his pistol and squeezed the trigger.

Leitrim peered from the safety of a protruding bulge of rock, and when he felt Rashid had that battle under control, he darted around the corner to find another entrance to the fort, and found himself in one of the walled animal walks. He hastened forward, around corners, only to find more walks. He finally came to a low, rounded door, tried it. It was locked, but gave way after half a dozen kicks from his booted foot. He went into a perfectly black corridor, that seemed to open like a maze in various directions. At one intersection, he saw a chink of light and ran toward it. The corridor led to a lighted area, with one man, holding a rifle across his lap as he sat, nodding.

His chair was propped against a closed door. Unless Duval had more than one prisoner, that had to be where Melora was being held. Leitrim crept forward, and frowned to see the guard was pale-skinned, like himself, and young—hardly more than a boy. It seemed a crime to shoot him. The boy heard a sound behind him and sat up at attention. The noise was repeated. Melora was pounding on the door. When the boy rose and turned his face to the door, Leitrim lunged forward and knocked him on the head with the butt of his pistol.

He quickly got the key from the hook and unlocked the door.

"Leitrim! It's you!" Melora exclaimed, and threw herself into his arms.

He hardly had time to glance at her tear-stained face. "Hurry. We've got to get out of here. Duval's men are coming."

He grabbed her hand, running toward the maze of corridors that had brought him to the place. Just as the fleeing couple disappeared around a corner, Duval's men found the unconscious guard, and the empty room. They shouted, pointing toward the corridors, and gave chase.

Their following footfalls echoed ominously. At every turn Leitrim hoped to see the rounded door leading outside, but it evaded him. He was trapped in the endless cobbled, fenced corridors, and the pursuers came closer. He pulled Melora into a dark corner. They waited with bated breath as two men ran past.

"They've escaped out the door!" one of the men called. "We'll follow."

Leitrim peered to see which way they went, then followed them at a little distance. The low, rounded door appeared around the next bend. Was it safe to dart out, or would their pursuers be waiting for them?

"We'll have to risk it," he said. "Are you ready?"

Melora gulped and nodded her head. Speech was impossible. They flew out. They saw their pursuers; one had gone in either direction. They rounded the corners of the fort and disappeared.

Leitrim grabbed Melora's hand and pointed toward the opening in the wall. "You'll find horses and two of Rashid's men a quarter of a mile down the mountain. Run, and don't look back."

"But what about you, Michael?"

"Rashid's in there. I can't leave him. Go, for God's sake. And tell them to bring the horses forward. Our only chance is escape. Duval has a hundred and fifty men. We can't outfight so many."

"All right."

She shot through the shadows, and disappeared around the corner. Leitrim drew a deep breath and turned back to face the fort, just as a handful of Rashid's men came pelting out. Rashid was behind them.

"We've quelled the first lot," Rashid said. "The others will soon be along. We've got to find Melora."

"She got away. Come on."

"She's safe? You're sure?" Rashid demanded.

"I sent her to fetch our mounts."

Rashid pulled Leitrim into his arms and held him a moment. When he released him, his eyes were glazed with moisture. "I will not forget this, Lord Leitrim. Michael," he said, questioningly. "You permit?"

"I am honored, Rashid."

"All brothers under the skin, yes?"

"Dead brothers if we don't get out of here."

They ran together, laughing, down the mountain.

Chapter Fifteen

Lady Melora's hair was disheveled; her gown was in tatters and her face was dirty, but her eyes sparkled with joy. "It was splendid, Trimmer!" she said, as she sat with her rescuers, sipping tea in Rashid's European salon. Leitrim had set aside his *burnous* and wore only his shirt and trousers, but Rashid was still in his black robe. "And I was right all along. The white-faced man we saw at the *souk* with Duval was one of his pirates. Herr Gimmel turns out to be a Frenchie, Alphonse Lalonde."

"Then you mean *Monsieur* Gimmel, my dear. Everyone knows a Frenchie is called Monsieur. But what's in a name after all?"

Melora was not amused at having her story interrupted and continued impatiently. "He's the one who guarded me in the cell. He tends the fort when Duval is away."

"What I cannot understand is why you went pelting off in the night with Duval. And not leaving us any notion where you had gone. You knew Leitrim's opinion of the man."

"He had promised to take me to see a mosque," she explained. Rashid scowled; Leitrim glared, and Miss Trimmer tsk'd ineffectually. "But I wasn't going to go with him. I only went to tell him I *wasn't* going. It seemed impolite to leave him waiting after he'd gone to the bother of arranging horses and everything."

"You ought not to have done it," Trimmer said, but not so firmly as a chaperone should. "I thought you had only sneaked off to meet one of Redding's officers, as you used to do occasionally in India. And that was plenty bad enough, Miss."

Rashid's scowls grew darker. Noticing it, Melora quickly changed the subject. "What will happen to Duval?" she asked.

"It was necessary to kill him," Rashid said indifferently. "With him gone, the men who were with him will return to their fish nets and herds of sheep."

Trimmer nodded pensively. "It was very naughty of you, Melora, but all's well that ends well. And now we really must retire. It's four o'clock. If you will excuse us, Rashid."

"I shall accompany you to your chamber," Rashid said, and with a jealous eye to Leitrim, he rose to take Melora's arm.

Leitrim stopped him. "Let them go. The ladies have had enough excitement for one night," he said, "and I would like just a moment of your time."

Rashid looked uncertainly toward Melora, who

was yawning into her fist. "I daresay it can wait till tomorrow," he replied, but rather testily.

They watched the ladies leave, then Leitrim said, "About the truce—"

Rashid waved an imperious hand. "There is no need for a truce now. We have broken up Duval's pirate ring. I shall take over the fort at Raz-al-Khaimah. My friendship with England is not in question."

"We still haven't caught Rahma b. Jabir."

"He will be less trouble without Duval to supply him with ships and information."

"There are other pirates about as well. My assignment was to get your signature on the truce, and till I achieve that goal, I feel bound to remain with the Bombay Marines. My three-year term is up. I would be free to return home if—"

Rashid's eyes narrowed suspiciously. "This is the first I have heard of your returning to England, milord. Is there a special reason for it at this time?"

"There won't be another company cruiser leaving for a month."

"Even then, Lady Melora will not be on the ship," Rashid said knowingly. "She will leave on the first one, or not at all. I shall 'sleep on it,' as you say."

"The ship leaves tomorrow."

Rashid gave a start of surprise, that soon assumed a tinge of anger. "So soon? Why did you not tell me this earlier?"

"For reasons of security. It was Captain Redding's order."

"This is a peculiar way to treat an ally."

"Till the truce is signed, Your Excellency, we are only friends, not allies."

Rashid studied his companion. "Even friends, when they compete for a prize, are rather tentative friends."

"We mustn't allow a lady to interfere with duty to our respective countries."

"You prefer to my betrothal to Shaikh Amir's daughter? That is my duty." Rashid sighed wearily. "How naive the British are. Ladies always interfere. Tell me, will Lady Melora's reputation remain intact after this affair? It is my understanding that an English lady's reputation is most fragile. To hear such shocking stories of her slipping away to meet officers—and to desecrate a mosque with her presence!—no gentleman would marry such a lady. Is it your hope to make her your mistress?"

A blaze of anger flared swiftly in Leitrim's eyes, but he tried to quell it. "I wouldn't dream of making an improper offer to a lady of impeccable virtue."

"Nor I, milord. But you must own the lady's reputation is hardly impeccable, whatever of her virtue."

"As Lady Melora's protector, I must take issue with that."

"Another time, perhaps. Now I shall leave you, Leitrim."

Rashid studied his opponent from narrowed eyes. Then he turned and strode from the room without saying goodnight. Leitrim stood a moment, thinking, before he hastened up to the ladies' apartment. He knocked lightly at the door.

Miss Trimmer, in a dressing gown and with a cap over her curls, opened it to him.

"What is it, Leitrim?"

"I must speak to you. I fear the *shaikh* may be planning something rash."

"How you slander the poor man. He is unexceptionable."

"Would you still think so if he made Melora an offer not of marriage, but a *carte blanche*?"

"He'd never do such a thing!"

"Would he not? I'm afraid I must make very certain he toes the line. I don't want to have to call him out."

"What do you mean?"

"I shall offer for Melora myself. He's gentleman enough that he won't insult my fiancée. Have I your permission, Trimmer?"

Trimmer's eyes lit up at this suggestion and she fell into a twitter. "To tell the truth, I have been hoping you would. it would be the icing on the cake, Leitrim. And silly people say you can't ice your cake and eat it too. I'll just get her—she isn't in bed yet. And even if she is . . . use the balcony, Leitrim." She darted toward the balcony door, then turned back. "So romantic, with that fat, yellow moon—you can't miss. She'd accept an offer from a butcher with that moon shining on her. Not that I mean to say. . . . She is in excellent spirits too. She's been speaking of your heroism in glowing terms. How her heart lifted when Rashid came darting to the rescue. 'I was never so glad to see anyone in my life,' she said."

"Rashid?"

"Oh and *you*. She mentioned you too, Leitrim."

Trimmer called Melora, then discreetly disappeared into her own chamber. Lady Melora, caught unawares, had pulled a lace peignoir over her nightgown. Dressed all in white, she appeared to Leitrim as a bride. His eyes softened at the vision.

"What is it, Leitrim?" she asked impatiently. "As you can see, I was about to go to bed."

He glanced to the balcony, where the moon lent the atmosphere he wished for the meeting. "Shall we step outside?" he suggested.

She lifted her hand to her lips, stifling a yawn. At close range, Leitrim saw she was dead tired. Purple smudges had appeared below her eyes, and her expression was wan. Perhaps the moon's benefit could be invoked without actually going outdoors. "Nice moon," he said, to call her attention to it.

She gave it a passing glance. "Very nice, and soon it will be the sun. What on earth is so important you must say it tonight?"

Leitrim swallowed once or twice, and when he spoke, his voice sounded hollow, devoid of passion or any feeling. "Melora," he began woodenly. "I haven't had the honor of knowing you very long, but the circumstances of our acquaintance have been peculiarly intimate. I have come to respect—admire you."

Her only response was curiosity. "Thank you, Michael. I respect you too. You and Rashid were very brave tonight. You both looked so dashing in those black *burnouses*. I shall hint Rashid into wearing a black *burnous,* from time to time."

"Don't be ridiculous," he scoffed, angry at her

changing the subject, particularly to Rashid. "A black *burnous* would be hot as Hades in this climate."

"Not at night."

"I didn't come here to discuss Rashid's wardrobe!"

"Good. That is hardly important enough to keep me from my bed," she snipped. "What is the earth shattering confidence that can't wait till morning?"

"I want you to marry me," he said, almost angrily.

Melora regarded him suspiciously. "What are you up to?" she demanded. "You don't love me. You don't even like me."

"Of course I do," he barked. "Why else would I be willing to shackle myself to you for life?"

"What a charming prospect! I don't know why, but I suspect it has something to do with your precious truce. I will not be used! How dare you insult me with an offer like this!"

"Insult you!" he exclaimed. "Well, upon my word! You should be flattered! You may think you'll cut a dash when you go home with your tales of *shaikhs* and kidnapping, but you're sadly out in your reckoning. I doubt if a single polite salon will be open to you."

She tossed her shoulders. "Then perhaps I shan't go home. I may decide to accept Rashid's offer instead." She peered from under her lashes to read the effect of this threat.

"You had best wait and hear what manner of offer he plans to make before you say that. Don't count on its being an offer of marriage, after tonight's escapade. And a few other escapades Trimmer was indiscreet enough to mention in front of him.''

''I was practically engaged to Charles when I slipped out that night in Bombay to meet him. We only walked in the garden. And nothing happened at the fort. I mean nothing that a gentleman would consider damaging to my virtue. Naturally that is all that concerns you. That I was bound and kidnapped and thrown into a mouldy old cell, frightened for my very life, counts for nought, as long as my precious virtue remains intact.''

''A gentleman's wife must be akin to Caesar's in that respect. Not only virtuous, but above any suspicion. I promise you, Rashid is rethinking his offer.''

''And as you are not, am I to assume you don't consider yourself a gentleman?'' she asked pertly.

Leitrim drew a deep breath and counted to ten. ''I didn't come here to argue. Will you marry me or not?''

''Certainly not. And I've finally figured out what you're up to. You know perfectly Rashid's going to offer for me, and you don't want me to marry him. That's all. You're willing to sacrifice yourself to show the world you did your duty in protecting me from a perfectly charming, rich, powerful man, who adores me.''

''You overestimate Rashid's infatuation. He adores Allah. He lusts after you. *Shaikhs* don't necessarily marry every woman they happen to covet—only four of them.''

''We shall see! And now I thank you for the honor you have done me in making this halfhearted offer, Lord Leitrim, but I fear—"

"It isn't halfhearted! I do love you," he said, but the expression on his face looked more like hate, or at least anger.

Melora studied him a moment. Michael was really rather sweet. And there were certain obvious inconveniences to being marooned in the desert, away from the delights of England.

"You have an odd way of showing it. I'm tired. Good night, Michael." She flounced into her chamber, and Lord Leitrim put his hand to his forehead.

"Ass," he muttered to himself, and left.

When he had gone, Trimmer leapt from her bed and hurried forward. "Did you accept him?" she asked eagerly.

"No."

"Why ever not! He is so eligible, my dear. I made sure you would snap at the offer to attach Drumcliff's eldest son and heir. You should have discussed it with me before turning him off. Two heads are better than none. You'll not get a better offer in England I promise you."

"No, not in England, perhaps."

Trimmer gave a tsk of disgust and returned to her bed. Melora opened the door to the balcony and walked outside. Why had Michael made that terribly gauche and ill-timed proposal? It was unlike him to be so awkward. Did he really love her?

There was very little sleep taking place in Shaikh Rashid's castle that night. Melora's kidnapping and rescue left a residue of excitement that refused to be dissipated. Leitrim stood at the window of his room, berating himself for his wretched proposal. He hadn't even convinced her he loved her.

Shaikh Rashid sat in his private quarters, thinking, reading his richly-adorned Koran as he sought guidance in this problem. His eyes strayed to the hammered brass box that contained the pearls. They would always remind him of Melora. They had the same transluscent, creamy glow as her skin. How lovely they had looked around her throat.

He held them in his hand, and opened a door into the courtyard. Concealed by the shadow of a bush, he gazed up at her window, saw the light. As he stood gazing, the door opened and Melora came out into the moonlight. She looked like a fairy princess, all dressed in white. Goddess of the Moon! A gurgle of laughter sounded deep in his throat. He returned to his apartment, wrote a note, wrapped it around the pearls and had them sent to her room.

Five minutes later, Melora was interrupted by yet another tap at her door. The echo of it came to her faintly on the balcony. Michael! she thought, and hastened to admit him. It was a servant. He handed her the paper, bowed, and left.

"Please accept this token as an apology for the indignity suffered while my guest. Wear them for me, if you love me," the note said. It was signed with a bold, slanting R. Melora lifted the beautiful, smooth, cool necklace and stood staring at in confusion. She knew the pearls were worth a king's ransom. In her mind, a scrap of conversation echoed. 'These will be worn by your wife, when you marry, sir?' And the *shaikh's* enigmatic smile. 'Only by a lady of great importance, certainly. These are not a toy for a *houri*.' Not a *houri*—but he hadn't said wife.

She fingered the smooth pearls thoughtfully. It was Michael's warning that put these wretched ideas into her head. Of course Rashid wanted to marry her . . . but did she want to marry him?

She fastened the necklace around her throat and studied herself in the mirror. The long rope of pearls hung over her bosoms. How well they looked with the white lace of her peignoir. She would wear them with white lace. Michael would be furious! A soft smile curved her lips as she imagined his anger if she should wear them tomorrow. That would teach him to come storming into her room, making an offer of marriage that sounded like an order.

Any hope Melora had of sleep after her strenuous night's activity was lost by this new development. She went again out to the balcony and gazed up at the moon. The same moon that was shining on her old friends at Bombay, on the ships at sea, and her relatives in England. She felt close to them all, as though her past life was drawn together by the moon's beams. With a wistful sigh, she placed her hands on the stone baluster. She noticed a peculiar, soft roughness against the stone and looked down to examine it.

A stout hemp rope hung to the ground, its end held in place by a grapple inside the railing. Duval! was the first thought that was in her mind. He had planned to come up here after her if she failed to keep their appointment. Obviously no one used such a secretive means of getting to her if his intentions were honorable. She touched the cold iron of the grapple, but it was firmly imbedded; it would take a man's strength to pull it out.

But Duval was dead now, so the danger was

past. She was about to go back inside when she discerned a movement in the shadows. The thing was so dark she thought at first it was only a bush swaying in the breeze. Then it moved more noticeably, detached itself from the shadows. It was a man, striding in a leisurely way toward the rope. As he came closer, moonlight shone on him, revealing Rashid's proud walk, his arrogant brow, the planes of his aquiline nose, the sculpture of his cheeks. He looked up and smiled a reckless, abandoned, frightening smile. It told her who was responsible for the rope.

Melora emitted one fierce shriek before taking to her heels. As though led by instinct, she flew straight to Michael. Leitrim turned in astonishment as she flung open the door and threw herself into his arms. He noticed her agitation, then he noticed the pearl necklace. Then his arms closed around her, and he noticed only the soft curve of her body pressing against his, and the subtle scent of jasmine that came from her hair. For a moment they clung together, till her trembling had subsided.

"You were right, Michael," she gasped. "He didn't mean to marry me at all. He was climbing up my balcony."

"Where did you get the pearls?" he asked.

"He sent them to me with a note." She handed him the note, still crumpled between her fingers.

Michael read it and gave her a questioning look. "Why did you wear them?"

"I was only trying them on. I had no intention of accepting them."

"Rashid must have misunderstood when he saw them on you."

Her eyes were large and dark with fear. Her

fingers moved in agitation against his shirt front. "What shall we do?" she asked.

"If I were your fiancé, I would call him to account," he suggested. Mischief danced in his eyes. "As matters stand now, all I can do is tender a stiff reprimand on behalf of the East India Company."

He read an answering smile. "That's blackmail, Lord Leitrim!"

"So it is, Lady Melora. You see how your influence has depraved me." He frowned and became more serious. "Truly, Melora, I do think the safest thing is for us to pretend we're engaged till you're safely out of here. Rashid's efforts may not stop at one try."

Her lips pulled into a pout. "Pretend?" she asked. "Then it was all politics, your offering for me? You didn't really mean—"

"I meant every word!" he said earnestly. "I meant lots of words I didn't say, too. Darling, I love you. I should have said that first, and we might not have fallen into argument."

"Are you sure, Michael?" she asked, and looked anxiously for his answer. "You're not just worried about my safety?"

"I wouldn't be in a cold sweat about your safety if I didn't love you. I wouldn't have arranged with Redding to captain his ship, the ship holding you—to England if I didn't love you."

A smile like the rising of the sun lit her face. "You're coming home too?" she asked.

"Soon, darling. Very soon. I intended to accompany you if I could get Rashid to sign the truce."

"And if I had decided to remain?"

Michael cupped her chin in his fingers and lifted it till she was gazing into his eyes. His words were harsh, but his eyes were tender, full of love. "Then it would have been more imperative than ever that I put an ocean between us, or I would certainly have declared war against the *shaikh*," he said, and lowered his head to kiss her.

For a moment, she was lost in the ardor of his embrace. She had chosen the right man, a man whose life and way of thinking she understood completely and had no reason to fear. His hot lips moved restively, possessively on hers as he crushed her against him. A warm wave of love engulfed her. She felt the brush of Michael's fingers at her throat and raised her hand to hold his. The pearls slipped from her neck, and she knew that Michael had unfastened them.

"I'll return these to Rashid for you, to save you the embarrassment," he said.

Melora pulled the strand through his fingers. "He gave them to me. I shall return them tomorrow—discreetly."

"And firmly!"

"Very firmly," she agreed, smiling. "My fiancé disapproves."

"I'll tell Rashid so when I speak to him. I'm going to do it tonight, or we'll neither of us get any sleep. But first, I'll remove that grappling iron."

They went together to Melora's apartment. She watched while he pulled out the grapple and yanked the rope up. The same moon shone down. It seemed to smile as Leitrim stole a quick kiss.

"If Trimmer is still awake, I'll tell her about my engagement," Melora said, rubbing her cheek against his shirt front.

"That's *our* engagement, Melora. You will remember to mention it is I you're marrying, not Rashid."

"Of course, darling Michael. How strange! I shall have to start thinking of someone else besides myself. You must forgive me if I occasionally make a slip."

"I'll be sure to remind you," he said. The echo of lilting Irish laughter hung on the air as he left.

Chapter Sixteen

"So you accepted an offer from Lord Leitrim. I cannot tell you how happy I am," Miss Trimmer exclaimed, and went on not telling of her pleasure for several excited minutes.

"That's two weddings—first Ayesha, now me," Melora said. "Good things come in threes, Trimmer. You'll be next. I believe Captain Redding has eyes for you."

"Don't tell me you believe that foolish superstition that three is a lucky number!" Melora was surprised that her chaperone should steer clear of superstition. "Everyone knows seven is the luckiest number," Trimmer added, with an air of great authority.

Melora yawned as she sipped her morning coffee—not for boredom at her new engagement, but because she had had only three hours sleep. It was now eleven o'clock. Trimmer had slept in till ten-thirty.

"What a pity we cannot land in England with him by your side. But there—Rome wasn't built without straws. He will soon join you."

"Perhaps he'll come with us."

"Oh my dear, nice as the *shaikh* is, I cannot like to think of battening myself on him for another month, till the next company ship passes. I really think we ought to accept a ride with Captain Redding. And that reminds me, the packing!" She leapt from the table and went into the bedroom.

Melora sat on. Once she was alone, she pulled from her reticule the pearl necklace and gazed at it. The pearls were perfectly matched. They glowed with the iridescense of opals—pink and blue and green glinted from their creamy surface. When a knock sounded at the door, she quickly stuffed the necklace back into her reticule.

It was Lord Leitrim who came in. He had made a careful toilette. His face was freshly shaved, his linens immaculate and every button on his uniform twinkled, but it was at his left eye that Melora stared. It wore a bruise as big as a man's fist and the color of a trout's back—all gray and purple and glistening. "Michael! What happened?" she demanded.

"What, this?" he asked, touching it gingerly. "I—er, bumped into a door last night."

Melora lifted an unbelieving brow and said, "It had a powerful right hand."

"Left. And if you think this is bad, you should see the other door."

"Did you actually come to blows with Rashid?"

"First words were exchanged, then insults. Once

you've offended a *shaikh*, you may count yourself fortunate to get off with only your daylights darkened. It was unfortunate. In fact, it was damned stupid of me, but I didn't want to call him out, and couldn't let him off Scot free after—Well, enough of that. We shook hands like the gentlemen we are when it was over, but the resentment is bound to linger. Much chance I have of getting his signature on the truce now. I've been replaced as the negotiator. I've just come from Captain Redding."

"You've been up that long?" Melora asked.

"I was in something of a hurry to get matters settled. He agrees with me that today is the safest day for the Reliant to leave port. The pirates will be in confusion with Duval gone. They won't mount an attack on the ship, so we're leaving this afternoon. He's appointed Officer Warworth to continue the negotiations, and I shall escort you ladies back to England. I hate to leave with my mission unaccomplished," he said, and drew a deep sigh. "And I shan't be getting Sinbad now either. Rashid promised him to me if we carried your rescue off successfully last night." He discreetly refrained from using such words as 'unharmed,' or 'alive.'

"He won't renege on his promise. Rashid is a gentleman."

"We shall see. And you, my love, being a very proper young lady, must return the pearls."

"He called them a token, to make up for the indignities suffered by one of his guests."

"He also asked you to wear them—if you loved him."

Melora sighed resignedly. "I suppose I must

return them.''

"Certainly you must, and the sooner the better. We'll go and look for him now. It will be best if I not go into his apartment with you. The sight of us together might cause his anger to return.''

"I should prefer to be alone with him," she said. "I wonder if he really meant to seduce me last night, or it was just a romantical gesture. We had spoken of the balcony, and Romeo and Juliet.''

"We'll never know—will we?''

"I must know, Michael. That's why I wish to see him alone. Will you take me to his apartment now?''

"Very well.''

"I shall just freshen up first," she said, and disappeared into her room.

It was a quarter of an hour before she came out, carrying the pearls. Leitrim noticed jealously that her eyes sparkled and her cheeks were bright with excitement. Less obvious to him was that she had carefully arranged her hair and perfumed herself with Rashid's favorite scent.

They went together through the echoing corridors. At Rashid's trellised door, Leitrim knocked and a servant answered. He handed Lord Leitrim some folded sheets of paper. Leitrim read the top sheet, then glanced at the bottom one and gave a hoot of delight. "The truce! He's signed the truce! Good God, I was sure he'd withhold it from me. That was well done of him.''

The servant smiled and spoke again. Leitrim looked positively sheepish when he translated. "He says I'm to have Sinbad.''

"You must thank Rashid, Michael, but after you've done so, leave us alone for a moment.''

"Oh, did I not tell you? Shaikh Rashid has left for his summer palace," the servant said.

Melora's brow puckered. She drew her bottom lip between her teeth, and felt an overwhelming pang of sadness and loss. There were so many things she had wanted to say to him. Now she'd never know just what Rashid's intentions had been.

"You can leave the pearls," Leitrim suggested.

"Yes, I shall."

She went alone into the sparsely furnished room, looking all around, storing up memories. Rashid's ornate copy of the Koran was open on the inlaid table where she had often seen it. She took the pearl necklace from her reticule. It slid slowly through her fingers, to form a luminous puddle of circles beside the book.

The afternoon sun was lowering as the Reliant left the harbor. From its stern, Melora, Trimmer and Leitrim gazed back at the coast. Palm trees looked like little black umbrellas, but the shaikh's castle still loomed large. It shone like an enchanted golden castle in a fairytale. Everyone knew fairytales weren't true. They were just a romantic illusion, to beguile an idle hour. Reality was Michael, and Trimmer, and England.

Melora turned her back on the receding view. "Well, Captain, will you permit your fiancée to take the helm for a moment?" she asked.

"Don't permit it, Leitrim," Trimmer said firmly. "She'll have us aground before you can say Jack Robinson. Where is your pantry? I want to make a nice cup of tea. There is nothing so satisfying as a nice cup of tea when one is feeling upset.''

Leitrim smiled at his fiancée. His fingers closed possessively over hers. "I can think of something finer,'' he said.